# RATTLESNAKE ROCK

## A TIME-SPANNING THRILLER

## MARCUS WILLIAMS

WILLIAMS & CO. PUBLISHING

WILLIAMS & CO. PUBLISHING

# FOREWORD

This story contains depictions of domestic abuse, sexual assault, alcohol abuse, and violence. While I refrained from using graphic depictions of those scenes, it is impossible to speak of the horrific experiences of a victim of violence without describing the manipulation, emotional trauma, and physical harm perpetrated by the abuser. If you or someone you know is suffering from abuse, please know that you are not alone. There are people around you who will understand and do anything they can to help and protect you. For help, call 1-800-799-SAFE in the United States. My phone is always available to anyone who needs it to call for help.

# Preface

## Circa 700 AD

D espite weeks of solitude, the screams of his people and the clash of swords constantly plagued him.

As a scholar and a scribe, he was charged with documenting the never-ending wars of his people. It seemed that all of the tribes had taken one side or the other in this war. Except, despite the passion and carnage they all embraced so openly, he still couldn't figure out what they were fighting for.

It was as if they were fighting simply to die, to destroy centuries of civilization for no other reason than to see if it were possible.

They moved often, trying to stay ahead of advancing forces. But each day they left more of their people behind, victims of this senseless hate. Was it because his God somehow hated their gods? Or had God left them to their own devices, washed His hands of them?

Their numbers grew fewer and fewer until it was just him and a young girl. She had latched on to him for some reason when the last of her family died in battle, so he watched over her and let her share his fire and food.

But now, even she had left him. As far as he knew, he was the only one of his people left. Soon, there would be no one. For days, the others pursued him through the forests and across the open plains. He carried only a scroll to write on and a sword to protect himself. Otherwise, he traveled light, moving mostly by night and hiding during the day.

As the landscape changed, his pursuers fell further behind, until one day he realized that he hadn't seen or heard them for at least a week. Still wary, he continued his pattern, traveling on foot through rough country previously unknown to him or his people.

He took to describing the land in his scrolls. He no longer had anything else to write about. His people were gone, lost to time, recorded only on the scrolls he carried with him. One day, if he ever found a place to rest, he intended to transfer the record to plates or tablets, something that would last longer.

He traveled day after day in the direction of the setting sun, and found himself one day entering a wide valley. Water had grown scarce, and it had been days since he had crossed a river or a stream. His waterskin was so dry he feared the leather would begin to crack as badly as his lips. He sucked on a pebble just to create enough spittle to swallow. He knew he would die if he didn't find water soon.

He walked into the valley, marveling at the sparse and unfamiliar vegetation. His home had been rich and green, the grass so high you could get lost if you weren't careful. Large lakes filled with fish were fed by rushing rivers cascading down from the mountains. The land was full of game, and food grew abundantly in its season. The people had lived in prosperity and peace until the wars came.

They had been happy, or so he had thought.

Standing sentinel in the valley, a column of rock stood alone, like an altar to God constructed by a race of giants. He approached warily, as it was nothing like he had ever seen before.

He saw strange tracks on the ground, unfamiliar animals that must inhabit this barren place. The valley was quiet, and his heart raced with trepidation. Slowly, he unsheathed his sword, his eyes darting left and right, alert for any sign of danger.

As he got closer to the rock, he saw the sweeping tracks of a serpent in the sand. He slowed his pace, knowing that a serpent could be dangerous or at the very least, a bad omen. He walked up the bank of a dry gulch and stopped suddenly when a rattling sound broke the silence. He scanned the valley, but saw nothing. He took a cautious step forward and the rattle grew louder and more intense. He froze.

From under a rock, a snake emerged, its black eyes boring into him. At the end of its coiled body, its tail shook, and he realized it was the source of the sound. What was this creature who could sing?

The snake's forked tongue flicked in and out. He grasped the hilt of his sword tightly as his palms broke out in sweat. Would he be fast enough if the serpent struck?

"You are thirsssssty, traveler," a voice hissed.

"Who's there?" he cried.

"It isss me," the voice said.

He looked down at the snake in unbelief.

"Follow me, and I will lead you to water," the snake implored.

He felt keenly the dryness in his throat and his swollen tongue.

The snake slithered away, then looked back as if asking if he was going to follow.

He took a step forward before the voice of his mother filled his mind.

"The serpent will beguile you. It is a trickster."

He could see himself as a boy sitting around the fire as his mother taught him and his brothers.

"Quickly," the snake hissed. "I will quench your thirssst,"

He stepped forward as if to follow the snake, but at the last second, twisted his arm and slashed down with his sword at the same moment that the snake struck.

He adjusted his aim and jumped backward as his sword slashed cleanly through the serpent's neck. Its body coiled around itself and rattled. Its head landed cleanly at his feet.

He breathed a sigh of relief.

He cut the rattle from the snake's body and stuffed it into his pack. He set out in a run towards the standing rock, falling to his knees at its base. He bowed his head in the sand, hoping it truly was an ancient altar.

"Even if it's not, it can be," he said.

He looked to the heavens. "Oh God," he began, "quench my thirst as I protect the record of Thy people." He bowed again and then repeated the prayer over and over until eventually exhaustion overcame him. He fell into a deep sleep.

He was awakened by a cool touch on his cheek. He opened his eyes, sideways to the world, and lay still for a moment, trying to understand what he was feeling. He pushed himself up and stared in awe as a cascade of water fell over the edge of the rock to the ground where it soaked into the soil. The mist encircled him.

He rushed to the cascade, cupping his hands under the flow of water. He drank deeply until his stomach was full, then dropped to his knees to give thanks.

# CHAPTER 1

## 1849

Rose Callandish leaned against the crooked door frame, ignoring the sweat soaking through her blouse and dripping down her back. She watched as the wagons lurched ahead into clouds of red dust; she fought against the anger building in her chest.

Captain Adams frowned and cleared his throat. His paint mare stood next to him and whinnied as though she feared being left behind.

"You have your rifle, and we tucked your food barrels back against the rock face. You should be fine until the next company drives through." He wiped his forehead with his sleeve, leaving a smear of dust. He looked down and kicked at the dirt.

Rose didn't respond. They both knew it was too late in the season for another train to come through. For some reason, they both held up the pretense that help was imminent.

Bethany Dillon, Rose's best friend in the company, glanced over from her wagon as it passed the makeshift cabin and gave a tentative wave goodbye. She frowned and wiped a tear from her eye. The others did their best to look the other way.

"Mrs. Callandish, we all decided this was for the best. Your husband isn't fit to continue on the trail and with your condition..." He glanced down at her swollen belly. "We're already late as it is. The weather may turn at any moment, and then all of us would be stuck."

Rose refused to look at him. She had trusted him when, in Missouri, Adams had promised he would see her little family safely to Santa Fe. "You've said as much ten times. You needn't rationalize your broken promises to me again." She turned and walked inside.

"But Mrs. Callandish, Rose, please, we have no other option. Paul is snake bit and wouldn't survive the rough ride in the back of a wagon. You know that as well as I do. It's his only chance. There are frequent travelers on the road. If Paul survives..."

Rose whipped around, fire in her eyes, and advanced towards Adams with an arm poised to strike. He took a step back.

"I, I mean, of course he will...survive I mean. I didn't intend to...It's just that we can't wait any longer for him to get better."

"Just leave, Captain Adams. You've done enough." The creaking sound of wagon wheels and rusty springs outside drew her mind back to the first day on the trail when she and Paul looked at each other with excitement for their future out west together. He had helped her up onto the wagon bench with an exaggerated bow.

*"Your carriage awaits, your highness,"* he said while bowing deeply.

*"Stop it,"* she replied, giggling. *"What will everyone think?"*

*"That you are the queen of the company, madame. As they should."*

*"Just get in, silly. You're embarrassing me."*

*Paul grinned widely.*

Captain Adams coughed and replaced the sweat-stained felt hat on his head. "We'll see you both straight away in Santa Fe. I'm sure of it."

Rose nodded curtly, dismissing the Captain for the final time. He mounted his horse and looked down at the open door once again before kicking the mare's flanks.

Rose stood deathly still. A shaft of light drew a line across her sunburned face where sunlight shone through the cracks of the hastily built shelter. When she was sure Captain Adams was gone and that the last of the wagons had finally passed, she dared to move.

She could see the dust cloud in the distance where the wagon train reunited with the main trail, but the air around her was silent and oppressive in its heat. They had been camped there for a week, but she decided to explore the area further now that it was empty. The camp seemed entirely different without her friends and companions.

The cabin, if it could be called that, was crudely built from their wagon box. The men of the company had all joined in to piece together the ramshackle structure. The canvas acted as their roof, covered in hardened mud for insulation and protection from the sun. One of their guides had learned the trick from the natives south of Santa Fe. They mixed desert grass with the mud and then caked it over the taught canvas. The guide had wanted to use the same method to fill the chinks in the cabin, but water was scarce and they didn't know how long the natural water basin up in the standing rock column would last.

They built the cabin up against the rock face because they only had lumber enough for three sides. They stuffed the gaps between the side walls and the rock face with grass and did the best they could to anchor the little structure to the rock.

"It'll last until the next wagon train passes by at least," one of the men had declared, as if trying to convince himself.

Rose walked around the base of the cliff until she reached the narrow trail that led up to the catch basin. They had only found it because their guide knew to watch for bees. When one buzzed his ear, he eagerly searched until he found a narrow crevice leading up to the rare source of water. But there didn't seem to be any spring feeding the basin. Sheltered from the sun, the water would evaporate slowly, but even so, Rose knew the water would only last for so long. They needed rain to refill it if they were to survive.

She continued her climb to the top, where she could look out over the valley. The rock formation stood alone, surrounded by miles of nothing but creosote bushes and the rare juniper. Cholla cacti and yucca plants punctuated the steely landscape. She could see dust on the horizon from the wagons, but otherwise, she was completely alone.

She stood there for a time, trying to force down the panic fighting its way to the surface. Her husband lay dying of a snake bite down below, and her belly grew more each week. By her calculations, the baby would come soon.

Unable to contain her emotions any longer, she lashed out, yelling at the deep blue sky to whomever was listening. No one was there to witness her weakness. She had nothing left to prove.

"What have I ever done to You?" she screamed. She thought of the words her father, a traveling preacher, had taught her from the scriptures. "Why hast Thou forsaken me?" she cried. Tears streamed down her cheeks. A raven screeched overhead as if in reply. The sound wasn't comforting.

# CHAPTER 2
## 2024

Rosaria latched the deadbolt and shivered. The wind rocked the trailer and whistled through the ill fitted windows. She could feel the thin floor vibrate through her socks as the trailer shook on its cinder block foundation.

She glanced over at the microwave—11:48 pm. He would be home soon. Her heart raced in trepidation, but she forced aside the hurt and fear, allowing anger and indignation to take its place. She had done nothing wrong. No matter what he said; it wasn't her fault.

She yawned as she slumped into the worn couch. The springs were so worn, she practically sat on the floor. He had promised he would buy her a new one with last month's paycheck. She had even found one online that was in good shape and for a good price. When she had built up the courage to show the ad to him the Saturday morning after payday, he had reacted as he always did. At least this time the bruises were hidden under her shirt sleeves. She had done what she always did when he got that way and hurried to the kitchen to cook for him—that time it was eggs over easy just as he liked them, fried in bacon grease.

She was so tired. Her thoughts swirled around in her mind, unable to find purchase. She had planned her escape so many times, but had never been able to go through with it. Her sister had practically given up on her. But where would she go? The trailer was so far out of town with only one dirt road in and out. He never let her drive, and she had let her license expire anyway. His sister Soledad picked her up everyday to drive her to her job at the dollar store with strict instructions not to make any detours.

With her luck, if she ran he would find her before she even got to town—or she would die in the desert. Some days, that seemed like the better option.

There was a sign in the women's restroom at work with a number for women in her "situation" to call if they needed help. What phone did they think she was going to use? Didn't they know that he checked her phone every night? Unless they were prepared to swoop in and take her away on a moment's notice, the number just taunted her. Freedom was nine digits away, yet impossible to reach.

She reached over and picked up the cheap brass frame from the side table. It hadn't always been this way, although looking back she blamed herself for not seeing the signs. He had been so attentive at first. When he insisted on picking her up from work every night, she had thought that he was just being gallant. When he punched that guy in the restaurant for hitting on her, he was protecting her. When he bought her a cell phone and put her on his plan, he was just helping her save money. Every insidious act had an innocent explanation. He just loved her so much that he couldn't stand to be away from her.

Eventually, her friends gave up trying to call her or invite her to go out. He worked so hard all week and just wanted to spend time with her on the weekend. Why would she want to be away from him when he did so much for her? Couldn't she see that he couldn't live without her? But whatever she did or however hard she tried, it was never good enough for him. And then he moved her to a strange town where she had no friends.

The photo in the frame had been taken on their honeymoon to Albuquerque. She kept it next to the couch, because those were the last good days—the only good days really. He had been so carefree and loving that weekend. The hotel was a cheap one, and they took extra food from the hotel breakfast so they wouldn't have to pay for lunch. They spent the days in the hotel room or wandering through Old Town making up stories about the type of tourists who would buy the fancy jewelry sold in the shops lining the plaza. They laughed and held hands like a normal couple.

But then, a month later, when she missed her period, the honeymoon phase ended abruptly.

"How dare you get pregnant now. Do I look like I can afford your stupid little rugrat? What's wrong with you?" He spouted such ridiculous accusations so frequently that she started to believe it really was her fault.

She set the framed photo back on the side table and placed a hand over her empty womb. A tear trickled down her cheek and she choked back a sob. "It will be two years ago next week," she whispered.

She heard tires crunch on the gravel drive and could smell the rich exhaust of his pickup truck seeping through the seams of the trailer, carried in by the wind. She wiped the tears from her cheeks and pushed to her feet. It wouldn't do for him to find her sitting on the couch when he was sure to be hungry and expecting food to be ready for him, as if she could divine the exact moment he would stumble home from the bar.

She rushed to the kitchen and set water to boil. The doorknob rattled in its frame and she felt a moment of panic.

"Oh no," she hissed. "I locked the door and forgot."

She rushed over to the door but was too slow. He pounded his fists against the aluminum frame, surely denting it even more than it already was.

"Open the door!" he yelled over the howling wind as he kicked at the frame with his steel toe boots.

She fumbled with the lock, struggling to turn it as he continued to pound. Finally it clicked open and she turned the doorknob. The door flew open in a gust of wind just as his foot was about to make contact. His leg swung forward, the momentum carrying him over the threshold. He tripped, falling forward into the couch. He caught himself on the armrest and managed to stop his fall. He turned to where Rosaria stood trembling.

"Who's here? Who are you hiding?" he yelled. "You lock me out of my own house?"

"Nothing, nobody," she stammered. "The wind was going to blow the door open, so I locked it and forgot."

"Liar," he hissed. His breath reeked of cheap booze, and his eyes were red and glassy. He grabbed her by the arm and squeezed. "Take me to him." He pushed down the hallway into their empty bedroom where he threw bed covers and clothes to the floor.

"You're hurting me," she cried. She could feel the familiar bruises already starting to form on her arm.

Ignoring her, he pushed her to the second bedroom, the one she hadn't entered since that day. He threw open the door and stormed inside. The mobile over the crib shook and bits of a lullaby played mournfully. He let go to search the tiny closet.

Suddenly, he realized where they were and his focus shifted. "Wait a minute. I told you to clear this room months ago. Did I stutter, you lazy cow?"

"No, I'm sorry. I just..."

"I work all week and you can't even follow simple directions? Are you stupid? Did I marry an idiot?"

He raised his hand to strike, and she cowered against the second hand changing table. "I can't," she whispered.

He stared at her with contempt before deciding she wasn't even worth striking. He dropped his hand and grunted. "You'll do it now. Don't come out until it's done." He stepped back into the hallway, pulling the door closed behind him.

"No, please!" she wailed. "Don't!"

He slammed the door shut in her face as the teapot whistled in the kitchen.

# CHAPTER 3

## 1849

Rose sat down on the rock ledge, her feet dangling over the side. She had to admit, the desert held its own kind of beauty in its stark vastness. The color palette of dusty browns and deep reds was in such contrast to her life before, where the seasons were marked in shades of summer green, autumn leaves, winter snow, and spring blossoms. Back home you couldn't see a hundred yards in any direction because of the thick forests. Here, you could see forever.

She was born in the mountains of North Carolina, but her father had moved the family to Missouri when she was a baby so that they would be closer to his route as a traveling preacher. He was a penitent man who lived in a world of black and white. Any mistake was a sin that required harsh punishment and immediate repentance. He would be gone for weeks at a time, and when he returned, he would lavish them with love and attention at first. But after a week or so of being surrounded by his children and familial responsibilities, he became antsy and began to hear the call of God to spread the word once again.

They settled in Independence and built a good life there. Rose's earliest memory was a traumatic one of contention and violence outside their home. She had fleeting memories of playing with her best friend Becky Hyde in the front yard when a crowd of angry men marched down the street, led by her father.

*"Come inside girls," her mother said. She stood in the doorway, urgently motioning for them to come to her.*

*"But we're playing, Mother."*

*"You can play inside. Come on. Hurry."*

*Rose couldn't remember ever seeing her mother look so worried.*

*"I have fresh bread."*

*At the mention of a treat, Becky was the first to get up and go to the door. "Come on, Rose," Becky said. "I want bread."*

*"Good girls," Rose's mother said as she shut and barred the front door. She brought them into the kitchen and cut a slice of bread for each.*

*"Butter, mama," Rose said.*

*Her mother took back the piece and spread butter across the top before handing it back. "Do you want butter too, Becky?"*

*"Yes, please."*

*"Girls, I need you both to go upstairs to the nursery and play there, alright?"*

*"I want to go back outside," Rose protested.*

*"Not today, dear. I want you to just play inside."*

*"Becky, you can sleep here tonight. You can borrow Rose's old nightgown."*

*The girls' eyes lit up at the prospect of a sleepover.*

Rose was too young to understand what happened that afternoon but she remembered that not long thereafter, Becky and her family disappeared and the relationship between Rose's parents soured.

It wasn't until she was a few years older and overheard some ladies gossiping at the mercantile over a basket of yarn about a place called Nauvoo, that the memories resurfaced.

*"Serves them right, I say," one of the women said.*

*"They seemed like nice people to me, a little strange, but nice," another woman replied.*

*"It's awfully cold to be setting out across the river. They should at least allow them to wait until spring."*

*"And let them grow stronger? I disagree. The people need to do what we did here and rid themselves of the problem altogether."*

*Something the women said jogged a long-lost memory, and visions of little Becky hiding with her in her bedroom resurfaced. Rose was overcome with curiosity and approached the women.*

*"Excuse me, but may I ask of whom you are speaking? I apologize but I couldn't help but overhear."*

*"Why, the Mormons, of course," Mrs. Peterson replied. "You're the Sanders girl aren't you?"*

*"Yes, ma'am."*

*"Yes, I thought so. You'd be too young to remember the Mormons when they lived here I think."*

*"I believe you're right," Rose replied. "Thank you."*

*She turned and walked away, struggling to recapture the memories of that day.*

*She went straight home and found her mother working in the garden.*

*"Mother?"*

*"Yes, Is everything all right?"*

*"What really happened to my little friend Becky Hyde?"*

*Her mother stood and wiped her dirty hands on her apron. She sighed. "Little Becky? I haven't thought of her in a long time."*

Rose snapped out of her daydream and realized the sun was hanging low in the western sky. "I need to check on Paul and make some dinner," she said as she gathered her skirts and stood. She carefully climbed from the rocks, walked past the pool, and traversed down the narrow trail to the valley floor.

She entered the cabin and made her way to the dark corner of the small room where Paul was lying atop their makeshift bed of blankets and grass. He tossed and turned, sleeping fitfully. He was drenched in sweat and shivering. Rose pulled back the blanket to check his leg. The snake had struck him just above the top of his boot.

Paul had been walking beside the wagon to give his backside a rest from the bumpy ride on the hard wooden bench. They were the lead wagon that day, having been at the end of the train the day before where they were forced to eat and breath trail dust and horse manure all day. He was whistling a tune and didn't hear the warning rattle over the sound of the wagon wheels bumping over errant rocks.

One moment he was marching merrily along and the next he was screaming in pain from the snake's sudden strike. Rose pulled on the reins and jumped down to see what was the matter. Jeremy came running forward from the next wagon back and promptly shot the rattler before it could strike again.

The company medic cut open the wound and sucked out as much venom as he could while Jeremy's wife prepared a mustard poultice to pack over the wound. Paul rode in the back of the wagon the rest of the day, but by evening was vomiting and experiencing numbness in his face and hands. Captain Adams decided to pull the wagon train off of the trail to make camp.

Although they all pretended they were waiting for Paul to recover enough to continue, it was an unspoken secret that they were just waiting for him to die so that they could bury him and carry on. No one expected him to last the night, let alone a week. After a few days, the men of the party met together to discuss what to do, which is when they hatched the idea of building a cabin and leaving the Callandish family behind. No one had asked for Rose's opinion.

Rose peeled back the bandage and grimaced at his angry discolored shin. The wound was swollen and purple, yellowing around the edges. The sour smell of the poultice mixed with the puss seeping from the wound filled the little room with a foul stench. Rose grabbed a bottle of whiskey from where it sat on the barrel of flour and opened the cap. She didn't know how long she would need it, so to conserve it as much as possible, she placed a rag over the opening and quickly dipped it upside down. She dabbed at the wound with the alcohol soaked cloth, and Paul winced in his sleep.

"I'm sorry dear, but it is beginning to fester. I need to keep it clean."

After cleaning the wound, she stood and went to the makeshift table made from a trunk standing on its end with planks nailed to the top. She gathered the ingredients for the poultice and began mixing them in a copper bowl. The mustard powder tickled her nose, and she sneezed into her elbow.

The poultice prepared, she brought the bowl with her and knelt back down beside her husband. He opened his eyes a slit and smiled weakly.

"Hello, my princess," he croaked.

Rose took a cup of water and held it to his lips. He raised his head and drank. Water dribbled down the side of his face, and Rose dabbed at it gently with a corner of the blanket.

She set the cup down and got to work packing his wound with the poultice and wrapping it with a clean bandage. She was down to using strips of cloth torn from her Sunday dress as bandages.

"There, all done," she declared as she tied off the bandage. "Are you hungry? I have some stew from lunch still warming over the fire. I still can't believe Bethany's son got that jack rabbit."

Paul shook his head. Everytime he tried to eat, his stomach seized up in protest.

"How about a few sips of the broth, then? You've got to keep up your strength after all."

Paul smiled. "Of course."

Rose went to stand but Paul grabbed her hand in his. She turned back. "Is everything all right?" she asked.

"I love you," he whispered.

"I love you, too," she replied as she leaned down and kissed his cracked lips. "I'll be right back."

# CHAPTER 4

## 2024

Rosaria crawled to the door, sucking in mouthfuls of air between gasping sobs.

"Please, Jorge, no. I can't. Baby, please!" she cried. She reached up to turn the knob. With horror, she realized he had turned the knob inside out sometime before and had locked it from the outside. She pounded on the door. "Let me out. I'll cook you anything you want. Por favor, mi amor. Please, open the door."

Jorge didn't respond. She could hear him banging around in the kitchen. He was helpless in the kitchen on a good day but completely lost when he was angry and drunk. The teapot continued to whistle as he cursed.

"Jorge, let me help you. Please let me out."

She heard footsteps approach the door and crawled back in anticipation. Instead of opening it, he pounded his fist on the door and yelled, "Shut up you stupid whore." He punched the door again for effect and stormed away down the hall.

Rosaria collapsed on the floor. She felt herself beginning to hyperventilate and tried to focus on slowing her heart rate.

"Please, let me out," she gasped between breaths. "Please. Dios mio, por favor, let me out. Don't make me do this" Out of habit, she reached for the crucifix she had worn around her neck since her first communion. But her neck was bare. She squeezed her eyes shut and tried to block out the memory when he had ripped it from her neck and thrown it from the truck window because she had asked if she could go to mass on Sunday while he was out hunting.

Despite the missing crucifix, she began to recite the Rosary and eventually was able to calm her breathing.

At least the lights are on, she thought. She shouldn't have. As soon as the thought formed in her mind, the room went dark.

Jorge walked down the hall, slapping the bedroom door as he passed. "Maybe now you'll shut your mouth," he said, laughing.

She heard the toilet flush and the bed springs squeak as he fell into the old mattress. Soon, she could hear him snoring through the thin trailer walls.

Lit only by a sliver of moon light coming through the little bedroom window, Rosaria went to the door and tried to figure out how to get the lock to open. She knew that there was a way to open the lock through the little hole in the door knob, but had never done it or seen it done. In the dark, she scrambled to find something that she could use to fit in the hole but it was no use.

Clouds covered the moon, shrouding the trailer in complete darkness. With the nearest neighbor a mile away, no ambient light filtered through the bent aluminum blinds.

Finally, the exhaustion overtook her and she crawled under the crib with one of the baby blankets and fell asleep.

# CHAPTER 5
## 1849

T he three Apache scouts dropped down into the eastern edge of the valley out of the narrow canyon. They had patiently watched the wagon train from a ridge until it finally disappeared over the horizon. The standing rock was an ancient site, known for its life-giving water. It had been days since passing the last water hole, and their horses were in desperate need.

It had been difficult to sit still and watch the unwary travelers trespass on their land, but they were under strict orders to scout and report back—no attacks which would provoke the cavalry from Fort Leavenworth.

Their throats were parched from the long journey and lack of water, and with only three of them, they were no match for an entire wagon train, even if it was mostly made up of women, children, and farmers.

The lead scout silently gestured for his companions to follow and keep a lookout. They crossed the valley, dropping into a dry riverbed about halfway to the standing rock. The bed flooded during the spring runoff, but quickly dried out in the summer sun.

As they rode out of the depression, the lead scout stopped suddenly and his two companions rode up beside him.

He pointed towards the rock. They watched in surprise as a thin curl of smoke rose into the sky, very faint against the purple hues of sunset. Using hand signals to communicate, the three scouts separated in a flanking movement to come at the rock from all sides.

The lead scout quietly pulled his bow from over his shoulder and readied it in his right arm. He set down the reins and his horse reacted obediently to gradual pressure from his knees. As he got closer, he silently slipped from the saddle on moccasined feet and crouched low.

His companions did the same and waited for his signal to approach. His eyebrows arched when he saw the ungainly structure built against the rock wall, a new addition since they had passed by a month previous.

*Just like them to claim the sacred waters for their own*, he thought. *As if a person can own the waters.*

His blood boiled in rage at the audacity of the travelers. Usually, they were content to only pass through the valley, which was bad enough. But when they started building structures, that was a step too far. The chief would be anxious to learn of this intelligence.

With his orders not to attack in the back of his mind, the scout signaled to the others and dropped to his stomach behind a creosote bush to get a better picture of the opposition he was facing. He needed the water, but the occupants of the cabin stood in his way.

***

Rose stepped outside, preoccupied with worry for her husband. She knew the fact he had survived so long was a miracle but he didn't seem to be improving. *At least he's not getting worse*, she thought.

She placed a few sticks on the hot coals and blew gently until they caught fire. A cast iron pot hung from a tripod over the fire, filled with the last remnants of rabbit and snake stew. Rose thought it appropriate that they eat the beast who had attacked her husband without provocation. She actually didn't mind the taste.

The stew included a few beans, some wild onions she had collected back in Kansas, and simple dumplings made from salt and flour to make it more filling. She stirred the pot as it warmed over the fire and busied herself preparing a bowl.

Her stomach grumbled as the smell of the stew reached her nostrils. She felt the baby kick and placed her hand over her stomach.

"Are you hungry too, little one?" she said, laughing. "Be patient. It's almost supper time."

It was growing dark, and she could feel the heat being sapped from the earth by the sun's gradual exit. She questioned whether she should go back inside to let Paul feel the baby kick. That always revived his spirits. She turned to look back at the door and froze.

How had she not noticed it before? Someone had nailed the rattlesnake skin next to the door. It stretched from the top edge of the door frame down to the height of her knees, its dead black eyes staring directly at her. A slight breeze blew through camp, shaking the rattle ominously.

She stared at the vile creature in disgust. Who thought that she would want to be reminded of their predicament every time she walked inside? Was it some sort of cruel joke?

"I'll take it down first thing in the morning," she said as she turned back to the pot, trying to ignore the serpent, although she felt its beady eyes watching her every move. She ladled out a small amount and sipped carefully. It was done. She filled her bowl, leaving the ladle on a rock next to the fire, and went inside to eat.

It was too dark to see in the cabin, so she found a candle on the makeshift table and struck a match. The candle's dim illumination failed to reach the corners of the tiny room, but it was enough to eat by. She sat down next to Paul and carefully took a spoonful of broth from the bowl. She blew on it before holding it to his lips. He lifted his head and slurped the small portion. He laid back and smiled.

"The baby was kicking," she said as she took a spoonful for herself. "I think he's hungry."

"He?" Paul croaked, smiling. Paul desperately wanted a son, although he would never admit it.

"Or she," Rose replied.

"Or she," Paul repeated.

She gave him another sip.

"The wagon train left today," she said. "You were asleep, but they asked me to share their well wishes."

"Hmph," he grunted. "I could have made it."

"You can barely sit up," she replied. "Although it would not have hurt them to stay a few more days at least. It was Mr. Ledbetter who pushed them to get moving. He seemed very antsy about arriving late to Santa Fe." She paused. "Do you think another party will come through this season?"

"We can pray, but it's almost wintertime," he replied. He wasn't the type to sugarcoat things.

"My prayers are keeping you alive. I'm not sure I have a right to ask for more."

"Hmm."

She gave him another sip.

***

The scout watched the pregnant woman prepare dinner and return back inside the little cabin. *Is it a trap?* he wondered. There was no way they would have left a pregnant woman behind on her own. *There must be men in the cabin or keeping a lookout on the rock.* He signaled to his companion on the right flank to climb the rock to check.

His companion nodded and ran in a crouch to the seam in the rock. He didn't make a sound.

The scout waited, scanning between the cabin door and the rock until he saw a shadow emerge at the top. The shadow waved the all clear sign, then disappeared from view. Whomever they had left behind had to be with the woman in the cabin. When his companion reappeared and took up his position, the sun was just setting below the horizon, throwing a long shadow over the cabin.

The scout lifted his arm and gave the signal. With a hair-raising war cry, the three scouts descended upon the cabin, darting to their left and right to avoid any riflemen aiming at them through the gaps in the boards.

\*\*\*

Rose's heart jumped in her chest when the stillness of the evening was broken by the sudden blood curdling screams. She recognized the sound at once and her heart sank. It matched the stories she had heard along the trail perfectly.

After a split second of frozen terror, she lunged towards the rifle standing next to the door. Paul reached for the pistol lying next to him on the floor and pointed it at the open doorway.

The screams seemed to come from every direction, like a thousand warriors were descending upon them. The sound echoed off of the rock wall and reverberated through the little cabin. Rose's hands shook in terror as she readied herself to defend her little family. She looked over at Paul and he nodded his assurance.

She whispered a quick prayer as she brought the rifle to her shoulder. The screams grew so close that she expected the invaders to burst through the doorway at any second. She tensed.

Suddenly, the world fell silent.

Her heart was pumping so hard and fast that she could hear nothing else. She remained frozen, waiting for the attack to resume as she tried to control her breathing. The pounding in her ears retreated, and she began to hear whispers spoken in an unfamiliar language. At least two, maybe three distinct voices whispered urgently to each other.

She frowned and looked back at Paul. He shrugged but kept his pistol at the ready. After taking a deep breath, she stepped into the doorway, her finger hovering over the trigger. It took her brain time to process what her eyes beheld as she stepped outside. Three Apache men stood, pointing excitedly at the cabin. Confused, Rose looked to where they were pointing before remembering the snake nailed to the wall.

The three men noticed her standing there and stopped speaking. They dropped their hands to their sides but Rose continued to eye them warily, her rifle at the ready.

"What do you want?" she finally asked.

They did not respond.

"Do you speak English?"

They looked at each other and then the man in the middle finally spoke. "Powerful spirits," he said. He looked from the snake to her pregnant stomach and back to the snake.

"Powerful," one of the others agreed.

They stared at each other, Rose assessing her chances against three Apache warriors, and the men wondering what powerful medicine this white woman must possess.

Rose finally broke the silence. "My husband," Rose explained. "He was bitten."

The three men looked at each other and she realized that they probably didn't understand. She pointed at the snake and made fangs with two fingers. She pointed inside the cabin and then imitated getting bitten on the leg. Their eyebrows rose in understanding.

"Your man. He lives?" asked the apparent leader of the group.

"Yes," she said. "But he is very sick."

"When he...?" He mimicked her pantomime for being attacked, not knowing the word.

Rose thought for a second, counting the days in her head. She held up six fingers. "Six days. Six suns."

The scout gasped. "He lives?" he asked again.

"Yes," Rose repeated.

He pointed towards the door and raised his eyebrows.

Not really knowing why, Rose stepped aside and gestured for the three men to enter. The leader nodded and walked through the door. Rose followed and nodded to Paul, who still held the gun. Trusting his wife, Paul set the gun down at his side.

# CHAPTER 6
## 2024

Rosaria awoke to the sound of Jorge's plodding footsteps in the hallway. Disoriented, she felt a moment of panic at the closeness of the crib above her head. Her shoulder hurt where it had lain against the hard floor, and she felt the dry cotton taste in her mouth she hated so much. Slowly, she crawled from beneath the crib and pulled herself to her feet.

Usually, things always seemed a little better by day, but not this time. Just the sight of the crib and changing table made her heart catch in her throat.

Jorge swore in the kitchen and called out. "Where's my coffee, woman?" He stomped around some more. "Where are you now, you lazy cow?"

Rosaria hesitated, not knowing whether or not to respond. He had clearly forgotten what he had done the night before. She wasn't surprised. With his drinking, he frequently forgot. On more than one occasion he had very innocently asked her what she had done to get a black eye, never even considering it was his fist that had done the damage. On those occasions, she found it easiest to come up with some excuse. "Oh, it's nothing," she would say. "I was clumsy and ran into the doorframe in the dark when I was going to the bathroom."

"Clumsy ox," he would mumble. "Put some makeup on it before you go to work. You look horrible."

"Of course I will. Have a good day," she would say as she handed him his lunch box.

How would she explain the fact that she had locked herself in the baby's room last night and somehow switched the breaker off from the inside?

"Rosaria, where are you? I'm going to be late."

She heard the front door open, and Jorge called out again as if she would have reason to be outside in the yard so early in the morning. He finally gave up the search and trundled back down the hall. As he passed the bedroom door, he stopped as if something had triggered a memory.

She heard him jiggle the handle and laugh. "That's right," he said. "I almost forgot."

She took a step towards the door, nervous yet hopeful that he would let her out. He had never locked her in a room before; this was new territory.

"Did you get the room done?" he asked through the door.

"No, I uhm..."

"What? I can't hear you?"

"I'm sorry. It got dark before I could finish. There's no light."

He began to laugh, remembering how he had shut off the breaker to thet room. "Well, it's daylight now. So, get it done. I'm going over to Jimbo's to help him with the Camaro."

"Can I use the bathroom first? I really need to pee."

"I really need to pee," Jorge mimicked her.

"Please, Jorge. Then I'll get it done. I promise."

"Just hold it. Maybe you'll work faster."

She looked back at the crib. She had no idea what to do or how to take it apart. Didn't she need some sort of tool?

"Jorge, please. I need tools anyway. Just let me out and I will get it done before you get home."

He didn't respond but she heard his footsteps fade away down the hall. After a few minutes, he returned. She stepped back when she heard the lock being turned. Jorge opened the door and threw in a screwdriver, allen wrench set, and a bottle of water. The bottle hit her in the chest and she flinched at the impact.

"Get it done," he commanded and shut the door.

She heard the lock click into place.

At the sound of Jorge's truck roaring to life, Rosaria leaned down to pick up the tools.

"Soledad will be here soon to take me to work and she will let me out," she told herself. She breathed a sigh of relief.

Her phone was on the kitchen counter and there was no clock in the room, but she knew that Jorge usually left to help Jimbo every Saturday at around ten. They would putter around on Jimbo's '78 Camaro, working their way through a 24 pack of beer until the beer became more important than the car and they moved the party to the bar.

Her thin fragment of hope disappeared as quickly as it had formed. If Jorge was going to Jimbo's, that meant it was Saturday, and Rosaria wasn't scheduled to work today. No one was coming.

She dropped to the ground, criss crossing her legs, and rocked back and forth. *What do I do? What do I do?* she thought. She really did have to pee, and the more she thought about it, the worse the urge became. She picked up the tools to examine them. "Maybe he's right and it's time," she said, looking up at the crib.

The light blue blanket lay crumpled on the floor under the crib. "I must have grabbed it to sleep last night." She crawled over on the thin brown carpet and reached under the crib for the blanket. She held the soft fabric to her cheek and allowed the memories to flood over her. Tears began to soak through the quilted images of teddy bears and balloons.

Despite Jorge's anger at her pregnancy, Rosaria had been overjoyed. Despite everything Jorge did or said to her, she always knew she would have a sweet little one who would love her and need her. Maybe Jorge would see the baby and decide to change, be a father.

She began to prepare for the baby and saved every extra penny from her job to buy the crib and changing table from the local thrift store. One of the nurses at the clinic helped organize a drive to get her clothes and diapers. Every happy memory from that time had to do with preparing for the baby. It became her lifeline, the only reason she had to smile.

When she learned it was a boy, she was sure that Jorge would be happy to be having a son. Boy was she wrong.

Rosaria stood and ran her fingers across the worn wooden railing of the crib. "How many babies have you cradled?' she asked. She laid the blanket back down on the mattress and smoothed it out. "My little baby boy," she said, choking back a sob. "My perfect little boy."

It had been a rainy night, a monsoon like they hadn't seen for years.

*The trailer leaked and she placed pots and pans throughout the room to catch the dripping rain. The fat raindrops pounded on the thin metal roof until she couldn't hear herself speak over the noise. Wind rocked the trailer, flooding her mind with images of tornadoes ripping through trailer parks like she had seen on the news.*

*She felt a drop of water land on the top of her head and she instinctively looked up just in time for the next drop to land right in her eye. She wiped it away and cursed under her breath. She was out of pots. She felt a pain shoot through her back and put a hand under her swollen belly to support the weight.*

*She had become increasingly uncomfortable and unable to sleep. It hadn't stopped Jorge from making advances and getting ever angrier when she turned him away.*

*She went into the bathroom and slowly leaned down to pick up the little trash can. It was getting harder and harder to lean over. She took it back to the kitchen and found the wet spot on the floor where the new leak had sprung.*

*She looked over at the fridge and smiled. Earlier that day, she had snuck away from work on her break for an appointment at the clinic. It was just next door. The nurse had done a sonogram and happily announced that it was a boy. Rosaria was unsure how she could tell but believed her anyway. She carefully folded the print out and tucked it into her back pocket. Now it was attached to the fridge with the only souvenir from their honeymoon, a magnet from Albuquerque. Well, the only souvenir other than the baby.*

*Jorge tracked mud and water into the house when he got home from work, not caring to even take off his work boots. He smiled lecherously and enclosed Rosaria in a wet hug, his hands clumsily pawing over her body. Rosario flinched at his disgusting breath as he sloppily tried kissing her neck and fumbled with the buttons of her house dress.*

*"You're getting me wet," she protested.*

*He kicked off his boots, sending them flying into the cabinets. Mud splattered across the laminate surface.*

*She tried to push him away but he gripped her tighter.*

*"No, Jorge. Not now."*

*He didn't stop.*

*"Please, stop. Look, the roof is leaking, and you're wet…"*

*He managed to tear open her dress, popping off the last button and pinning her arms down at her sides as he tried to pull it off. Rosaria's heart raced and she felt panic rising in her chest. She couldn't move.*

*"Stop!" she begged weakly.*

*He growled and redoubled his efforts. "You're my wife," he grunted.*

*He backed her up against the kitchen peninsula. She was trapped.*

*She struggled against his groping, but had nowhere to go. Finally, she found her voice. "STOP IT!" she yelled, shocking even herself.*

*He paused, glaring at her, his eyes dark with rage and his hands still pinning her arms to her side.*

*"I have a surprise for you," she said desperately. "The baby, it's a boy. You're having a son." For some reason, she thought that would please him and possibly make him stop.*

*He growled and spoke in a terrifying tone that she had never heard him use before, so low she could barely hear him. "You deny me, your husband, and then dare bring up that little bastard?"*

*"But he's your..."*

*He brought a hand to her neck and squeezed. She gagged and struggled for air, but she couldn't breathe. She pawed desperately at his tightly clenched fingers, drawing blood with her nails. He growled in pain and lifted her onto her tiptoes, marching her towards the door. With his free hand, he yanked open the door. Rain whipped inside, soaking the exposed skin of her back.*

*"If you won't treat me like your husband, then why are you here?" He pushed her out the door, letting go his vice grip around her neck. She gasped, desperately trying to fill her lungs. His push spun her around. She reached out, trying to catch herself, but the old rusty*

*handrail gave way. She landed on her stomach on the edge of the cinder block stairs and then smacked her head against the engine block that Jorge kept in the yard to one day fix up and sell. The world went black.*

*She couldn't say how long she had been out, but when she awoke, muddy water streamed over her ankles. She rolled over, the rain still pelting her half naked body. She tried to blink away the dull throbbing in her head. As she assessed her wounds, she felt a sharp pain in her womb. She scrunched into a ball and screamed in agony, holding tightly to her stomach.*

*"No," she cried. "Not that. Please, not the baby." Another pain hit and she felt warm fluid between her legs.*

Rosaria gasped. She hadn't allowed herself to think about that night since the day Soledad had brought her home from the hospital. She had never even had a chance to see the baby before they took him away promising that she didn't really want to see him—that it was for her own good.

Jorge never said a word about that night, and Rosaria just closed the nursery door and never went inside again. Until now. Standing there with her hand on the crib, Rosaria finally faced what Jorge had done to her that day. In place of the grief she had buried for so long, she felt rage growing inside of her.

# CHAPTER 7

# 1849

P aul flinched when the Apache scout took the candle and knelt beside him on the ground. The scout studied him in silence before pulling back the blanket to look at his swollen leg. Paul winced when the scout began unwrapping the recently tied bandage, but managed to remain silent.

The scout grunted and wrinkled his nose at the smell. He removed the poultice, wiping it away roughly with the bandage. Tears formed in Paul's eyes from the pain but he was determined not to show any weakness. He looked up at Rose, and she shrugged. What was she supposed to do?

The scout motioned for his companions to join him and they conversed for a moment in their language.

Finally, the scout set Paul's leg back down on the blankets and turned to Rose. He pointed at Paul's leg and then up towards the rock face.

Rose frowned and shrugged. She didn't understand what he was trying to say. The Apache pointed again, this time adding the pantomime of pouring something over the wound. He looked back up at the rocks.

"Water?" Rose asked.

He grunted.

Rose went outside and returned with the kettle of water she kept by the fire. She held it out to the scout. "Water," she stated.

He shook his head and pushed the kettle away. "Water," he repeated but again pointed up at the rocks.

"I think he means he wants you to get him water from the pool in the rocks," Paul said, his voice raspy.

Rose pointed up at the rocks and then back at the kettle. "Water, from the pool?" she asked.

The scout nodded vigorously. He took the kettle from her hands and tossed the contents against the far wall before handing it back to her. "You go," he commanded.

Rose looked at her husband, hesitant to leave him alone with the three Apache men.

Paul nodded. "It's okay," he said. "Go."

"I'll be right back," she said.

She went to the doorway and looked back. The men were all watching her.

"Go," the lead scout repeated.

Rose made her way by the light of the stars and waning moon to the crack in the wall. She climbed quickly, the tin kettle banging against the sides of the thin crevice as she went. She emerged onto the ledge next to the pool. The still water reflected the moon and stars as clearly as any mirror. Rose felt hesitant to break the spell by dipping her kettle into the pool. She heard Paul cough down below and shook her head. She filled the kettle and carefully made her way back.

As she was away, one of the scouts retrieved their horses and brought them to the door of the house. He took a small pouch from his saddle bags and brought it inside just as Rose arrived. Rose handed the filled kettle to the scout and watched as he prepared a sweet smelling poultice with the powder from the little pouch.

He knelt in front of Paul, reciting something Rose couldn't understand under his breath. He then poured most of the remaining water over the open wound before applying the poultice. He indicated to Rose that she should not wrap the poultice with a bandage, but instead let it remain exposed to the air.

He then walked outside with the kettle and the others followed. He held his hands over the fire and instructed one of his companions to pour the remaining water into his open palms. He rubbed his hands together, letting the water drip and sizzle on the hot coals. Finally, he approached the snake pinned to the wall.

Without touching it with his hands, he peeled it off with his knife and carried it draped over the blade to the fire. He lowered the snake into the fire, careful to keep the rattle out of the coals. He set the rattle down on a rock in the fire ring and swiftly cut it from the rest of the snake.

The snakeskin crackled and hissed in the flame while the four watched. The scout took the rattle and presented it to Rose with both hands. She took it, trying to hide her disgust. She had no interest in keeping any part of the vile creature. But afraid to offend him, she tucked it into her pocket.

"Big medicine," the Apache man said, pointing up at the rocks.

"The water?" she asked.

"Big medicine water," he replied.

Without another word, one of the men retrieved a water bladder from each horse and disappeared into the darkness in the direction of the water. They stared at each other without speaking until he returned, the bladders full.

Rose felt like she had to explain herself somehow. She pointed back inside at Paul. "When he's better, we go." She pointed in the direction the wagon train had gone earlier that day.

The lead scout picked up a stick next to the fire. He pointed at the moon and then drew it in the sand. He drew an arch with the full moon at the top of the arch and a copy of that night's moon at the other end. He looked at Rose with a serious expression and then pointed down at his drawing. "One moon," he said as he mounted his horse. The others followed. "One moon. You go," he said before making a signal for death that Rose was sure to understand.

Rose gulped and nodded. She instinctively placed a protective hand over her swollen belly. "We will go," she replied. "One moon."

He grunted and clicked his tongue, turning his horse and trotting west into the blackening night.

# CHAPTER 8
## 2024

Rosaria studied the tools Jorge had thrown into the room, first picking up the screwdriver and then the allen wrench set. She walked to the door and examined the little hole in the doorknob. The screwdriver was clearly too big, so she tossed it onto the floor behind her. The allen wrenches were arranged in descending order of size in a plastic case. Rosaria chose the smallest wrench and carefully freed it from the case.

She had no idea what she was doing, but was determined to free herself. She pinched the little wrench between her thumb and forefinger and inserted it in the lock. She moved the wrench around inside the space, hoping to happen upon whatever it was that would unlock the door. She felt the wrench hit up against something straight inside the hole and she pushed at it from all sides to no avail. Finally, she matched the tip of the wrench with the tip of the center piece in the lock and pushed. She heard the lock click and her heart leapt in her chest.

Holding her breath, she carefully placed her hand around the cold metal of the knob, closed her eyes, and turned. The door creaked open.

Rosaria knew that she had heard Jorge's truck drive away down the gravel drive, but she still felt nervous at somehow being caught escaping from the bedroom. She silently crept through the house, checking every hiding place to assure herself that she was alone. When she had convinced herself that Jorge was truly gone, she grabbed a backpack from the hall closet and carried it into her bedroom.

"Where am I going to go?" she asked herself. When she felt especially lonely, she often resorted to carrying on conversations with herself. It helped her think and work through her feelings.

"You could go to your sister's."

"That's the first place he'll look."

"True. Well, you can't go to anyone in town. They would all give you up to him in a heartbeat."

"Except Melanie at work."

"Yeah, but Melanie is as broke as you are. She can't do anything to help you."

"What about the hotline number?"

"What are they going to do? The nearest shelter is hours away, and anyway, you remember what Jorge said he'd do if you ever try to go there. You can't put the other women in danger."

"So then where? I can't stay here. I'm done."

While she talked, Rosaria stuffed the backpack with a change of clothes, toiletries, and the pocketknife from Jorge's bedside table. She took the backpack into the kitchen and opened the cupboard.

"It sounds like you only have one option."

"What's that?"

"West."

"Through the desert? Are you kidding? I wouldn't know the first thing about survival in the desert."

"Don't you remember your girl scout days? You learned all about building fires and staying warm."

"That was in third grade." She laughed dryly.

"It's better than nothing."

"Not much."

After adding a package of jerky and a box of granola bars to the bag, Rosaria filled her water bottle and clipped it to the D-ring attached to the side of the bag.

"It can't be more than a day or two's hike to the highway over the mountains. Get there and hitch a ride to Colorado."

Rosaria shook her head at the prospect. Leaving the bag on the kitchen counter, she walked over to the living room window behind Jorge's favorite chair. She pulled open the blinds and looked out across the expanse of desert behind her house. There was nothing but creosote and cacti from the trailer to the mountain range in the distance.

She glanced over at the rusted metal shed at the back corner of their lot. The back wheel of Jorge's dirt bike was visible protruding from the doorway. She thought about it for just a second before shaking her head. For one, she didn't know how to ride it. And two, he would be able to follow its tracks much easier than her own.

Her mind made up, she closed the blinds and turned around to look at the place she had called home for the past almost three years, the place where she had suffered, cried, and wondered if life was even worth it, where she had called out to God every second of every day for help. Today was the day, with His help, that she would free herself from that hell.

"Even if I die out there in the desert, at least I'll be free," she said. She could hear the quiver in her voice, but pushed her doubts away.

She returned to the counter and took a piece of paper and a pen from the junk drawer. She began a note to Jorge but stopped on the second sentence. She desperately wanted to declare her independence and tell him she was leaving him for good, but felt the nagging sensation that wasn't the right move. Any claims of freedom from her would only anger him more. What she really needed was a diversion that would delay him for a day or two.

She ripped her first letter from the pad, crinkled it into a ball and stuffed it into her pocket. She began again:

---

Jorge,

My sister called and said she needed my help. She's picking me up and will bring me back on Monday before work. There are leftovers in the fridge and a pizza in the freezer.

Rosaria

---

She couldn't bring herself to write "Love Rosaria" at the end, even if the entire letter was a fake. She attached the note to the fridge with the magnet and sighed. It felt so final.

Satisfied that she had everything she could carry with her, she powered down her phone and hid it in one of the pots stacked in a cupboard under the counter. He would never look there.

She took her coat from the hall closet and stepped outside. She took a deep breath and looked up into the gray sky.

"God, if You're up there, I need Your help." She stepped down to the ground and started around the trailer. "I really, really, really need Your help. Amen."

# CHAPTER 9
## 1849

Paul's leg slowly healed. He no longer suffered from fever or chills, but the wound was still a sickly yellow. Despite the good news, he still suffered from numbness and tingling in his right foot below the bite.

He pulled himself to his feet while holding onto one of the food barrels, resting his weight on his good leg. Gritting his teeth, he slowly transferred his weight to his right. It was an odd sensation, being able to see his foot touching the ground, but not being able to feel it properly. It felt like he was stepping on pins and needles. Determined to trust his eyes, he shifted his remaining weight and let go of the barrel.

With a crash, his leg gave out and he tumbled to the ground in a heap. Rose came running inside at the noise.

"What was that? Are you okay?" she asked breathlessly. The baby pushed against her lungs and even the short run was enough to make her gasp for air.

"I'm fine," Paul replied as he turned himself over and sat up. "No harm done."

"What in the world were you doing?"

"I was trying to stand," he explained. "If we are going to get out of here, I need to be able to walk."

"I found something on my walk this morning," Rose said. She went to the doorway and reached just outside for the branch she had set against the doorframe. It was forked on one end. "I'm almost finished wrapping the top here to set under your arm and then I just need to measure and cut it to height."

With a grunt, Paul pulled himself up again, this time keeping his weight on his left leg. "A crutch? Where did you find that out here? There aren't any trees."

"Around the other side of the rock, there's an old piñon pine tree standing alone. This branch was broken off."

"How do you know what a piñon pine is, Missouri girl?" he teased.

"I pay attention and ask questions, unlike some know-it-all I happen to know," she replied with a grin.

"Oh really? Here, let me test that thing out."

Rose handed Paul the crutch and he fit it under his right arm. The length was perfect. He grabbed onto the shaft and took a hopping step forward.

"Not bad for a cripple," Rose declared. She appraised her husband as he tested the crutch. She felt a tear form at the corner of her eye and she quickly swiped it away when he was looking down. He was so thin and pale. His pants hung limply from his frame, his suspenders the only thing holding them up. His chest was sunken, and dark circles ringed his eyes. He had been so strong and confident when they had left Independence. Now he was just the shell of the man he once was.

Paul hopped over to her and smiled. He leaned in and kissed her on the cheek. She turned her face and kissed him back on the lips.

"It's perfect," he said. "Thank you."

She took his left hand in hers and smiled. "You need some sunshine. You look like a ghost."

"Doctor's orders?" he asked.

"Wife's orders," she replied.

"That's even more serious," he said. He made his way outside and squinted at the sudden brightness of the sun. He carefully lowered himself onto the little wooden camp stool next to the fire ring and exhaled loudly. He tried to hide his shaking hands from Rose, but she was too sharp.

"You just rest in the sun for a bit," she said. "I'm going to get supper prepared."

"Look at that," Paul said, pointing up into the sky.

Rose followed his finger and found the dim outline of the moon against the deep blue sky. It was close to full. The Apache's deadline would sneak up on them if they weren't watchful.

"It's beautiful," Rose said. She picked up their cast iron pot and went back inside. As she set it on the table, she felt a twinge of pain intensify in her womb. She gritted her teeth and breathed through the pain until it passed a few moments later. They weren't regular yet, but the pains couldn't be ignored. It was almost time.

"Are you okay in there?" Paul called out.

"I'm fine, dear. Just getting some flour out for the bread."

# Chapter 10

## 2024

The sky was overcast and there was a definite chill in the air. The high desert could be fickle in the early fall—cool one day and hot as July the next. Rosaria zipped up her coat and pulled on her light pink beanie.

She reached the edge of the backyard and stopped to look around one last time. Her life here had been miserable, but she had a bed, running water, a working toilet, and food. She would be giving up all of those things if she took the next step.

She hesitated and felt the urge to run back to the house and curl up in her bed. "Stop, Rosaria," she said to herself. "If you can survive Jorge, you can survive the desert for a couple of days. You can do this." With determination, she climbed over the sagging wire fence and walked out into the desert.

She walked for what felt like hours, but when she checked her cheap digital wristwatch, realized it had only been forty-five minutes. She walked up a rise and took a moment to take in her surroundings. From her trailer window, the desert looked flat and open, so she was surprised at the undulating hills, steep arroyos cut into the sand, and abundant plant life. She had found it impossible to walk in a straight line, and worried she was gradually turning away from her goal.

She looked off into the distance and found a dark spot at the top of one of the foothills in the distance. She couldn't tell what it was, but it seemed to be stationary. She held out her arm and pointed at the spot. Closing one eye, she peered down the length of her arm and evaluated her route.

"If I keep my eye on that spot, I should be able to travel in a straight line," she said. She turned to look back and was disappointed to see that the trailer was still too close. "Get moving, girl," she said. "You need to make it to the mountains by nighttime."

She unclipped her water bottle and took a swig before continuing her trek.

# CHAPTER 11
## 1849

The pains were still irregular and too much time passed in between for it to be time for the baby to come. Rose laid awake, staring at the ceiling in the gloom. Light from the full moon filtered into the cabin. She prayed for the baby to come quickly and especially that she would know what to do. It was her first, and she had little experience other than assisting one of the other women on the wagon train. The woman had suffered through a long and hard labor, and Rose had just done what the midwife told her to do while desperately trying not to freak out about her own upcoming labor.

Paul laid beside her. He snored softly, overcome by exhaustion even though he had spent the day sitting in the sun whittling.

"Oh, mother, I wish you were here," Rose whispered. "I don't know if I can do this."

She felt the urge to use their poor excuse for an outhouse, an all too common feeling these days. The air was chilly and she didn't want to leave the relative warmth of the blankets and Paul's body, but the urge refused to go away.

"This baby is a stubborn one," she whispered. She quietly grunted and rolled to her feet, careful not to wake Paul. She slipped into her shoes, something she wouldn't have worried about in Missouri. But it had only taken one scorpion sighting to convince her never to venture outside barefoot. Her jacket hung by a nail near the door and she grabbed it as she walked outside.

She quickly did her business by the light of the moon. As she was walking back to the cabin, she passed the small corral where they kept their team of horses. As she passed, they began pawing at the ground and snorting.

Rose looked out into the night, the moon casting long shadows in the distance, but bathing the front of the cabin in its cool glow. She squinted against the darkness, but couldn't see anything out of the ordinary.

The horses continued to snort and move around nervously.

Rose climbed over the rope fence and approached them. "Sshhh. What is it, girl?" She tried to stroke the mare's nose, but the mare jerked back. Rose ran her hand down the mare's neck and could feel her shaking. Rose had learned long before to trust her animals. Something was really wrong.

"It's okay, girl. I'll protect you," she soothed as she vainly searched across the landscape.

Various scenarios began to race through Rose's mind. Was it a human threat? Were the Apaches back, this time not so accommodating? Bandits? Was it an animal? Another rattler? She cursed herself for leaving the pistol lying next to her on the ground and the rifle next to the door.

She heard a low growl off to the left and strained to see. Another growl responded to her right. As she stared towards the sound, she caught movement out of the corner of her eye. She turned her head and found herself staring into a pair of white eyes floating in the night, a ghostly apparition unblinking and menacing. The creature behind the eyes growled and stepped out into the light.

The coyote bared its teeth and slunk forward, fixated on the two horses in the corral. Two others joined him and they advanced slowly, pinning Rose and the horses against the rock wall at the back of the corral.

Rose felt sweat drip down her forehead into her eyes despite the coolness of the night. Her heart pounded in her chest as she desperately tried to remember what to do. They had encountered other coyotes along the trail, but with so many people and so much noise, the mangy animals had always kept their distance from camp.

*What was it Captain Adams had said?*

The coyotes' guttural snarls sent the horses into a frenzy, creating as much danger to Rose as the attacking predators. She stepped away from them and found herself standing in the center of the corral with coyotes flanking her on all sides and panicked horses rearing up behind her.

*Noise!* She thought. *That's what he said. Coyotes are afraid of noise.*

"Hey! Get out! Go on. Get out of here," she yelled.

The lead coyote stopped and turned its head curiously.

"I need something to throw at them," she hissed. She tried to bend down, but found she couldn't reach the ground and still keep her eyes up to focus on the coyotes. She was too big.

The lead coyote yipped and the others responded as if they had decided collectively that this human's yells weren't a threat. It advanced.

Rose felt panic rising up inside her. She opened her mouth to scream, but nothing came out this time. Her throat felt dry and her tongue stuck to the roof of her mouth. "Paul," she managed to squeak. "Paul, help me."

She could have sworn the coyote grinned at her weak attempt to cry out.

"We have you now," she heard the coyote say in her mind.

She took a terrified step backwards and felt the hot breath of the panic-stricken mare against the back of her neck.

"Paul," she croaked, this time a little louder.

She reached into the pocket of her jacket, desperate to find anything she could use to defend herself or throw at the approaching animals.

> *"Coyotes are generally afraid of humans and loud noises,"* she
> recalled Captain Adams explaining as they all sat around the
> campfire. *"So just yell at them or throw rocks and they will run
> away."*

These three didn't seem to know that they were supposed to run away.

*"Towards the late summer, they sometimes can get a little more aggressive, especially if they are hungry," Captain Adams continued.*

Great, she thought. Just what I need—hungry, aggressive coyotes.

She felt around in her pocket and her fingers closed around a light papery object. Confused at what it could be, she pulled it out and held it up to the light. The coyotes took another step closer.

*The rattle*, she thought as she held the object up. Instinctively, she held the rattle by its tip and began shaking. Her hands were trembling so badly, it didn't take much. The ominous rattling sound filled the night. The lead coyote stopped suddenly and whimpered.

At the sight of the coyote's hesitation, Rose felt her voice return. "Heeyah, git," she yelled.

The lead coyote kept its eyes on her, but took a step backwards.

She shook the rattle harder. "Go!"

The three animals retreated further. Just as they were about to turn, a shot rang out in the darkness, echoing off of the back wall. The coyotes yelped in tandem and took off running into the night.

Rose looked over at the cabin and could make out the shape of her husband leaning against the door jamb with the rifle in his hands. She took a deep breath and stuffed her hands into her pockets. She clenched her fist and tried to force herself to stop shaking. As relief flooded through her, she began to laugh nervously. She felt the mare at her back, nuzzling her neck and chuffing its appreciation.

"You missed," she finally managed to joke.

"Are they gone?" Paul asked.

"For now," she replied.

"What was that rattling noise?" Paul asked.

Rose wrapped her hand around the rattle in her pocket. She hadn't told him about the Apache giving her the rattle. "Not sure," she responded, unclear why she didn't tell him the truth.

She could feel her heart rate returning to normal, and her breathing slowing. She checked on the horses. They stared at her calmly as though nothing at all had happened. She shook her head and chuckled.

She climbed over the corral fence and just as her back foot touched the ground, she felt a rush of warm liquid between her legs. She looked down and saw a dark patch of mud staining the ground at her feet. A pain, much stronger than any of the previous pains, washed over her. She clenched her teeth and bent over in agony.

"What's wrong?" Paul cried out. "Are you okay?"

Rose couldn't speak and held up one hand. She stood rooted in place, bent over in agony until the pain passed and she could straighten up. She looked over at Paul and felt the panic return. "The baby is coming," she replied weakly. "The baby."

# CHAPTER 12

## 2024

It was growing dark when she finally approached the base of the foothills. In the dusk, she could see that her guiding beacon on the hill was a small block walled building next to a cell phone tower. The light at the top of the tower blinked red.

She looked around to get her bearings and was surprised to realize that the sun had already disappeared behind the mountains; she was in the dark. She slung the backpack to the ground and bent over to unzip the top. She rummaged through the contents for the flashlight and pulled it out. She flicked it on and felt a twinge of panic. What if he could see the light from the cabin? She flicked it off again, unwilling to take the risk.

At the realization she was going to be stuck alone in the dark, her imagination suddenly went wild. Although she hadn't seen an animal all day, she had visions of coyotes and snakes stalking her in the darkness. She shivered and swore.

"Stupid, stupid," she hissed. She looked back up the hill. The small hut was now just a shadow against the night sky. Determined to make it to her goal, she carefully started up the hill, straining her eyes to see any obstacles in her path.

Low clouds covered the sky blocking any light from the stars. The full moon glowed behind the clouds, but didn't provide enough light to make out any detail.

"Ow!" she cried as she felt something stabbing at her shin. She ran her hand down along her leg and discovered a cactus spine sticking out from her pant leg. She tugged it free and stepped to the side hoping to avoid the plant further.

Gradually she scrambled up the hill to the building. It sat on a concrete pad surrounded by a cleared area of gravel. The phone tower nearby was protected by a chain link fence topped with barbed wire. She walked around to the back side of the hut and tried the door—locked. She heard a humming noise coming from inside the building.

She slumped to the ground, her back against the building, and rummaged through her pack in the dark.

She felt her fingers close around a plastic lighter and she brought it out of the bag. She rolled her thumb over the wheel, lighting the small flame, which did little to light the area. But it brought Rosaria a sense of comfort.

She leaned over and peered around the corner of the building back down into the valley. She could see the lights of their trailer off in the distance. Maybe it was just her eyes playing tricks on her, but she thought she saw a shadow momentarily block the window's light. She quickly hid herself back behind the building, extinguishing the lighter and hugging tightly against the block wall.

After a moment, her breathing calmed and she laughed at herself. "He can't see in the dark," she said. "You're safe."

She rummaged through her pack and pulled out the flannel blanket from the bottom. She covered her legs with the blanket and ripped open a granola bar. As she munched on the bar, her mind drifted to thoughts of the future.

\*\*\*

By noon that day, Jorge and Jimbo had managed to remove the Camaro's timing chain and work through a twelve pack of cheap beer. The Lobos football game started after lunch and they migrated to Jimbo's living room to watch the game.

Hours later, Jimbo sat snoring on his ripped vinyl recliner while Jorge went to the dirty bathroom to take a leak. He zipped up his fly and stumbled back down the short hallway to the living room.

"You have anything else to eat?" he asked.

"Huh, what?" Jimbo replied groggily.

"I said, do you have real food?" Jorge opened the fridge and stared at the moldy brick of cheese, carton of milk, and half-empty ketchup bottle. There was also one more bottle of beer sitting on the second shelf.

"Nah. I'm goin' shopping tomorrow." Jimbo pushed the lever on the side of his chair and sat up straight. He wiped his face with his sleeve and snorted.

"How about El Rancherito?" Jorge asked. "I could eat a burrito."

"Sure. Fine," Jimbo replied.

Jorge waited by the door as Jimbo used the bathroom and pulled on his boots. The restaurant was just down the road, and they walked.

"Hey, Maria," Jorge said as he walked inside. The bell above the door tinkled and a woman at the reception podium looked up.

"Hola, Jorge, Jimbo. Solo dos?"

"Unless you want to join us," Jorge quipped. "My treat." Jorge grinned.

Maria rolled her eyes and grabbed two menus from the slot on the side of the podium. "Follow me," she said, ignoring the invitation.

The restaurant was warm and filled with the scent of cilantro and the sound of seasoned meat sizzling on the grill. Jorge's stomach rumbled.

Maria showed the two men to a booth in the back and waited until they took a seat. She set a menu down in front of each of them. "Your waiter will help you shortly."

"But I want a beautiful woman like you to wait on me," Jorge said. He reached out to grab Maria's hand and she pulled away.

"Enjoy your meal," she said. She turned to leave and jumped in surprise when Jorge slapped her bottom. She paused, debating how to respond. She knew he was drunk and would just laugh if she protested, so she took a deep breath and walked away. "Pendejo," she cursed under her breath.

"What did you say, sweetheart?" Jorge slurred.

"Enjoy your food," she said without turning around.

Jorge swallowed the last bite of refried beans and belched loudly. A woman at the next table glared at him in disgust and he made a rude gesture with his finger. He picked up his tall glass and took another swig of beer. The table was riddled with empty bottles. Jorge picked up the most recent bottle and held it upside down over the glass. A single drop fell from the bottle.

"Uno mas!" he yelled.

Their waiter approached with an uneasy grin. "I'm sorry, sir, but the manager said that was your last drink."

"What? I'm a paying customer and I want another drink. What kind of dump is this?"

"I'm sorry, sir. Would you like your check?"

"Get me the manager," Jorge shouted.

The waiter looked over uncomfortably to the reception podium where Maria nodded her encouragement. "That's not possible sir. We need the table for another customer, so it's time for you and your friend to go."

"Come on, bro," Jimbo said. "Let's just go."

"Don't bro me," Jorge yelled. "I want another drink."

The entire restaurant was silent as the patrons watched Jorge make a scene. It was a small town and not the first time Jorge had gotten drunk and made a fool of himself.

Jorge stood up and got in the waiter's face. The waiter cringed at Jorge's garlic infused alcohol breath and took a step back. Jimbo stood and grabbed Jorge by the arm.

"Come on, dude. We can go to the bar."

Jorge snorted. He knocked the waiter in the shoulder as he stumbled to the front of the restaurant. Jimbo took out his wallet and threw a handful of bills on the table.

"Just let me know if that doesn't cover it," he told the waiter.

"Let's go, baby," Jorge said to Maria.

"Get lost," she replied. Jorge laughed and walked outside. "Anytime baby," he yelled over his shoulder.

"Poor Rosaria," Maria said. "What does that woman see in him?"

"Bar?" Jimbo asked in the parking lot.

"Nah, man, I should probably get home. See if the wife's done what I told her."

Jimbo laughed. "Yeah right."

They walked together to Jimbo's house and Jorge climbed into his truck.

"You good, man?" Jimbo asked.

"I'm fine. I've driven home worse than this before." It took Jorge several tries to get the key in the ignition. The truck roared to life and he shut the door. "Adios," he called and waved out the open window.

"Later," Jimbo replied as he walked to his front door.

Jorge backed out and pulled onto the main drag through town. He didn't notice the patrol car waiting in the shadows at the four way stop.

Officer Gonzalez yawned and checked his phone for the time. He was only a few hours into his shift, but he was already bored. Hopefully, things would pick up later when the bar closed. It was a Saturday night after all. He looked up just as a pickup truck roared through the stop sign.

"Finally," he said. He put the car into drive, checked both ways and turned onto Main St. behind the truck. The truck was floating from one side of the road to the other; Gonzalez recognized it immediately. "Son of a..." he swore. He flicked on his lights and whooped his siren once to get Jorge's attention.

Jorge looked in his rearview mirror and groaned. Surely, it wasn't for him. He pulled over to the side of the road to let the patrol car pass but to his surprise, it pulled in behind him. The officer flicked on the spotlight and shone it directly in his mirrors, reflecting the light in his eyes. He winced and shielded his eyes with his arm.

"What's the big idea?" he called out of the window.

"Get out of your truck Jorge," Officer Gonzalez ordered.

Jorge fumbled with the handle and stumbled out onto the street. He raised his hand to his eyes to block the light. "What's going on Santi?" he asked.

"You can't call me that when I'm working."

"Fine. Officer Gonzalez," Jorge said with exaggeration.

"You blew through the stop sign and were weaving all over the road. How much have you had to drink?"

Officer Gonzalez stepped closer and winced. "You smell like you bathed in a friggin' beer bath, man."

"I only had one beer," Jorge protested.

"Right, and I'm in the FBI." Officer Gonzalez sighed. Jorge was his godson, and he could let a lot slide, but not this.

"Fine. I'll leave the truck here and you can drive me home," Jorge said.

"No can do," Officer Gonzalez replied.

"What do you mean?"

"I mean, I got royally reamed the last time and the Chief said the law applies to godsons as much as anyone. I gotta take you in."

"Come on man. I didn't hurt anyone."

"You ever heard of zero tolerance?"

"Everyone around here drives after they've had a few. It's no big deal." He hiccuped and stumbled to the side. "Look, I can do all the tests." Jorge tried to balance on one leg and immediately fell to the side. He then began walking heel to toe, but ended up zig zagging until he was walking into the road.

"You can't even stand up straight and you just failed the tests. Come on." He led a grumbling Jorge to the back of his patrol car. "Do you have your gun on you?"

"Nah. It's in the truck."

"Great. Put your hands behind your back."

"Are you kidding me?"

"Arrest means arrest. I'm not going to lose my job because of you."

Jorge complied and sat grumbling while Officer Gonzalez belted him in. He watched as his god father went to the truck and rummaged around until he found the gun. He tucked it into his belt and returned to the driver's side.

"I'll hold onto this until you get out."

"When will that be?"

"Well, it's Saturday night, so you will have a hearing first thing Monday morning. Maybe you'll be sober by then."

"Monday? Ah man."

"Do you need to call Rosaria?" Officer Gonzalez asked.

Jorge thought about it and smiled. She'd be locked in the room until Monday just like he would be locked in jail. It would serve her right. "No. She'll be fine," he finally replied. He leaned his head back against the hard plastic seat and closed his eyes. This might not be so bad after all.

# CHAPTER 13

## 1849

Rose shuffled to the cabin, making it the short distance before the next contraction hit. Without thinking, Paul stepped forward to help her. When he shifted his weight to his right foot, it gave way and he collapsed, falling forward and knocking over the kettle of water she had filled to be ready for morning.

"That was the last of our water," she groaned. "The catch basin is almost empty."

"I'm sorry," Paul replied, wincing.

She noticed the pained look on his face and worry washed over her. "Are you okay?"

"Yes. I'm fine. I didn't think and landed on my good knee," he replied. "I'll go refill the kettle." He tried to stand using the camp stool as support. He only managed to collapse onto the stool.

Another pain washed over her. "No, you'll never make the climb," she grunted.

"But we need water for the birth. You said so."

"Yes, we do. Babies don't come immediately, so I'll go. We've got time. You build the fire up."

"But you..."

"We don't have any other choice," she interrupted.

With one hand clutched around her belly, Rose shuffled towards the break in the rocks. The pains were coming regularly, and she had to stop every few minutes to wait for them to pass. She leaned heavily against the crevice walls as she focused on taking one step at a time—one foot in front of the other.

"I can do this," she hissed through gritted teeth. "I'm not the first woman to give birth by herself. I can do this."

She finally reached the top, her nightgown drenched in sweat from the pain, exertion, and her waters.

"You're suddenly in an almighty hurry, aren't you?" she said to the baby. It responded with another contraction, this one bad enough that she collapsed to her knees. "Just hold on a little bit longer," she begged.

She began crawling to the edge of the catch basin. Without rain, the water level had slowly retreated every day. Earlier that afternoon, she had calculated there was only a day or two's worth left.

"Please be enough," she prayed as she crawled. "We just need enough for the baby."

She reached the edge and gasped in astonishment. Water sparkled in the moonlight, gently lapping at the top edge of the basin.

"Paul," she cried out. "Paul, it's full!"

"What? Are you okay?" he replied, his voice faint in the distance.

"I'm fine," she said quietly, in awe at the miracle before her.

"Rose, Rose, are you there? Can you hear me?"

"I'm coming down," she yelled. "I'm fine."

She filled the kettle first and set it on the rock. She then leaned down and cupped her hands together. She reached into the cool water and brought it to her lips, savoring the cool liquid as it flowed down the back of her throat. She took another scoop and splashed it over her face, basking in the refreshing feeling. A contraction brought her back to the present, reminding her that she did not want to have the baby up on the rock.

She crawled over to the step at the lip of the crevice and pulled herself up. She slowly began her descent down to the cabin.

As she emerged, Paul hopped over on his crutches. "I was getting worried," he said. "It felt like you were up there forever."

Rose smiled, feeling much more confident and ready for what was to come.

"You get this water boiling," she said. "I need you to clean the knife in hot water and get me some thread to tie the cord when the baby is born."

"Do you know what to do without a midwife?" he asked. "I've helped birth calves and colts before..."

"I am not a barn animal," she replied wryly.

"Oh, I, I mean, that's not what I meant," he stammered.

"I know. I'm teasing. I'll be fine. Women have been having babies since Adam and Eve, right?"

"Right. Okay, I will get the water on and bring you a blanket."

He turned to get to it but she grabbed his hand. "We're going to have a baby," she said.

He smiled and leaned in to give her a kiss. "Yes we are."

# CHAPTER 14
## 2024

Rosaria slept off and on throughout the night. It was colder than she had imagined; she jerked awake at the sound of every nocturnal animal scurrying through the brush. Her nerves felt frayed, and images of waking up with Jorge standing over her plagued her dreams.

She finally decided to get up when the world around her grew pink in the pre-dawn. She checked her watch and realized it was much earlier than she thought.

"I need to get going, anyway," she told herself.

She ate another granola bar and used a capful of water to brush her teeth. She spat on the ground and replaced the toothbrush in its little plastic container. She drank some water and hooked the bottle back on her pack. She ran her fingers through her hair, trying to work out the tangles from sleeping on a pile of clothes.

In the daylight, she was able to study her surroundings. A narrow dirt road led from the small building down into the valley. She studied her path and realized that in the dark she had cut up the steepest part of the slope when she could have used the road.

"Oh well," she said. "I made it, didn't I? That's what counts."

Morning mist settled over the valley obscuring the trailer. But she could see the living room light was still on.

"Jorge probably came home drunk and collapsed on the couch like usual. He probably forgot I was supposed to be locked in the bedroom and never even checked."

She slipped her arms into the backpack and planned her route down the back side of the foothill.

"He'll be checking soon though, and then all hell will break loose."

She thought about her sister. *After he reads the note, she will be the first person he calls, and when he finds out it was a lie, he will freak out.*

"Don't worry about me sis," she said to the sky. "I'm finally breaking free." She felt a twinge of guilt knowing that her sister would worry after Jorge's call.

Maybe she'll catch on and play along, she thought. Alejandra was smart and should figure out what was happening.

"Just tell him you will bring me back on Monday," Rosaria said as she climbed over a pile of rocks. "Give me another day. That's all I need."

\*\*\*

Word spread quickly that Jorge had finally been arrested for driving drunk instead of just being escorted home like usual. It was about time he faced some consequences before he ended up killing someone.

Maria heard the news first when a couple came into the restaurant after passing the arrest in progress. Maria walked outside into the parking lot to see what was happening and recognized Jorge's truck immediately. She grinned. "Serves him right," she said.

She returned to her post and, after seating the couple, texted Soledad to let her know her brother was going to jail. She could see that Soledad read the message, but she didn't respond.

Soledad showed up at the jail first thing the next morning and demanded to see her brother. The officer on duty sat back in the old office chair with his dirty boots propped up on the desk. He pointed to a sign hanging on the wall in response.

Jail Visiting Hours
10:00 - 12:00
Strictly Enforced

Soleded rolled her eyes. "Come on Brian. Just let me see him."

The entire building included the reception desk, an open area with two desks pushed together, a private office for the chief, an interview room, and two cells through a door in the back.

"No can do," Brian replied lazily.

They stared at each other, the only sound in the room the ticking of the clock on the wall until a snore from the back broke the silence.

"He's still asleep anyway," Brian said, shrugging. He dragged his feet from the desk and sat up. "Wanna coffee? I was just going to brew another batch."

"Seriously?"

"What? The rules is the rules."

"Since when?"

"I don't know what you mean." Brian stood and tugged on his duty belt. He sniffed and brushed some crumbs from his tan uniform shirt. "You sure? It's some new blend the chief brought in. It's pretty good."

"No, I don't want a coffee. I want to see Jorge."

"Ten o'clock," Brian responded, pointing back at the sign as if she hadn't understood the first time.

"Fine. I'll be back after church," she said.

Brian began preparing the coffee and heard the door slam behind him.

# CHAPTER 15
## 1849

"Ayyeeeeee!" Rose yelled into the night. She lay on the pile of blankets in the corner.

"If the coyotes weren't scared before..." Paul joked.

"Funny," she replied.

He sat next to her, lovingly wiping her forehead with a damp cloth and trying not to wince when she squeezed his hand during every contraction.

"I need to push," she declared. "It's coming."

"What do I do?" he asked.

Another contraction hit and she screamed through the pain. Hours had passed since she had returned from getting the water, and dawn was peeking over the horizon.

She tried to remember what the midwife had done at this point. "You need to catch the baby."

"What?" he asked, horrified.

"Catch the baby," she repeated.

"But I don't..."

"Don't what? Another one's coming. I need to push."

Paul scrambled into position. Rose gritted her teeth and groaned through the pain as she bore down. She didn't notice the look of terror on Paul's pale face.

"I see the head," he announced. "I see it."

Rose gasped in great heaving breaths as the pain subsided. "Here comes another one," she warned as she prepared herself to push again.

"Ayyyeeeee!"

Paul took the baby in his hands as a gush of fluid soaked the blanket. Rose laid her head back in relief, exhausted yet exhilarated.

"It's a boy," Paul announced proudly.

The baby lay motionless in his hands.

Rose felt alarm wash through her. "Why isn't he crying?" she asked. She pulled herself up onto her elbows to get a better view. "Do something," she ordered, fear suddenly filling her heart.

"What? What do I do?" Paul heard the panic in Rose's voice and realized something was terribly wrong.

"Give him to me," she ordered. She grabbed a blanket and held out her arms. Paul gingerly handed her the baby and she wrapped him in the blanket and vigorously rubbed his back. "Come on, come on," she urged.

Time stood still as Paul watched helplessly and Rose frantically rubbed the little boy's back.

"Please, God. Let him live," Paul prayed, finding he could do nothing else.

After what seemed like an eternity, the baby hiccuped and let out the sweetest sound Rose had ever heard. His little cheeks turned bright red and he wailed angrily.

Rose let out a sob and Paul realized he had been holding his breath. Rose began to laugh, and soon they were both laughing over the sound of the baby's cries.

Paul looked towards the heavens. "Thank you," he mouthed silently.

"Here, hand me the thread," Rose said as she tried to copy everything she had seen the midwife do.

The ordeal over, Rose sat exhausted on the bed, propped up with blankets against the back wall, the baby in her arms sleeping soundly. Paul followed her instructions to clean up and take care of the after birth. Finally done, he slumped down beside her. He leaned in and kissed his son on the forehead.

"What should we call him?" he asked.

They had happily discussed names as they traveled, but never settled on one. Rose couldn't bring herself to name him after her father and Paul had never known his father. She thought about their circumstances.

"He's our little miracle, isn't he?" she said.

"This is not what I had planned for us," Paul replied. "I'm so sorry."

"Why are you sorry?"

"We were supposed to be in a house in Santa Fe by now, with you in a big comfortable bed. But because I wasn't paying attention, we're stuck here in the middle of nowhere on our own."

"We're not alone," she said warmly. "We have each other, and we have God with us."

"I was praying like I've never prayed before," Paul admitted.

"I know. I heard you. And so did He."

"He did, didn't He?"

"Yes."

Rose thought back to her little friend in Independence and the bravery she and her family had shown in the face of angry mobs and persecution.

"Joseph," she said as she studied the bay's sleeping face.

"Joseph?"

"Yes. It's a good, strong, Biblical name."

"I was thinking of Moses or Joshua wandering in the wilderness."

Rose laughed. "Well, Joseph was taken to Egypt."

"I like it," Paul replied. "Hello, little Joseph," he said, brushing the baby's soft black hair with his fingertip.

He leaned in and gave Rose a kiss. "All we need now is a donkey and a manger to put him in."

Rose laughed harder and winced. "Don't make me laugh," she said.

"It's good to see you smile. It's been too long."

"I love you, Paul Callandish," she said.

"I love you too, Rose Callandish. And you, Joseph Paul Callandish."

# CHAPTER 16

## 2024

From her trailer, the mountains looked like nothing more than hills gently rising to the peak, easily climbed in an afternoon, But reality was much different, as Rosaria quickly learned. Instead of a gentle slope to the top, she found herself climbing up and down, scrambling over rocks and sliding down loose sand into dry creek beds.

She chose a tree at the top of the nearest peak as her reference point, but frequently lost sight of it in the narrow canyons. The sparse vegetation of the valley gave way to thick stands of juniper and piñon pines. Dry branches and pine needles scratched and pulled at her clothing and skin as she worked her way up the slope.

A jack rabbit darted away in front of her, alarmed by her sudden appearance. The air never seemed to warm, and she found herself hiking in shadow for most of the morning. She kept moving to keep warm and put as much distance between herself and Jorge as possible.

When the sun finally reached high enough in the sky to cast its light on the canyon floor, Rosaria decided to take a break for lunch. Her stomach grumbled in hunger, having worked off the granola bar long before.

She found a rock to sit on and shrugged out of her backpack. She held her face up to the sun and basked in its warmth. A bird chirped in a nearby ponderosa pine. She filled her lungs with the crisp, dry desert air.

A small stream trickled down the base of the canyon, but she could see the erosion along the bank where the waterline had been much higher during the spring runoff. Absently, she wondered why she didn't hike in the mountains more often. The idyllic scene filled her with a sense of calm and safety that she barely recognized. She hadn't felt like that for years.

She took some jerky from the pack and gnawed off a bite.

"I would have never known these canyons were here from the bottom looking up," she said. A squirrel curiously climbed down from a tree and stood on a rock across from her as if listening to what she had to say.

"From the bottom, the path looked smooth and easy—just like my marriage did."

The squirrel cocked its head to the side.

"The future was bright. We were supposedly in love. And I was unwilling to admit that the path would be a rocky one." She chuckled wryly. "Rocky is an understatement."

She took another bite of jerky as her thoughts swirled in her mind. She felt clarity for the first time in a long time. "But once you start the climb, you realize it's rocky, steep, and full of dangerous pitfalls. I'm halfway there, but I can't see behind me or what's ahead. All I can see is what's in front of me, right now."

The conversation was clearly too deep for the squirrel. It chittered its disapproval and scurried away.

"Maybe from the top, I'll see clearly." She took her bearings as she repacked her backpack to resume her hike.

\*\*\*

The door chimed and Brian looked up from his magazine and over to the clock as Soledad walked in.

"It's 10:30," Soledad said. "Visiting hours are open."

"I'm sorry, but it's Sunday," Brian began, trying to be funny.

Soledad didn't appreciate his attempt at a joke. She pushed through the swinging door to his side of the reception desk and marched toward the door at the back of the room.

Brian grabbed the keys from a desk drawer and hustled after her. "Woah. Wait up," he called.

She stood waiting at the door until he caught up, fumbling with the keys.

"He's the only one back there, so you can talk privately. Just knock on the door when you're done." The lock clicked and he pulled open the heavy steel door. "There's a chair there you can use if you want."

Soledad walked in without a word.

Brian closed the door and locked it behind her. "Witch," he mumbled as he returned to his post.

Soledad dragged the old wooden chair in front of the cell door and sat. Jorge was dozing on the bench at the back of the cell. The room reeked of stale beer, vomit, and urine. Soledad wrinkled her nose in disgust.

"Jorge," she called.

He mumbled something in his sleep and snorted.

"Jorge, wake up."

"Huh, what?" Jorge said, disoriented. He squinted his eyes and swung his legs to the side to sit up. He smacked his lips and frowned before rubbing his eyes.

"Jorge, it's me."

"Soledad?"

"Well, it's not Rosaria," she replied.

"You here to get me out?"

"You can't get out until you go before the judge tomorrow."

Jorge groaned, remembering that it was only Sunday. "Where's my truck?" he asked.

"Still parked on Main Street," she replied. "Luckily they didn't tow it. Why did you do it?"

"I was fine," he argued. "I was just driving home. My truck knows the way."

"Well, clearly you weren't fine according to Santiago."

"Santi, that hijo de... Bah, he could've just driven me home." Jorge ran his hands through his hair and walked over to the small stainless steel sink attached to the cell's toilet. He splashed water on his face and ran it through his hair.

"You were driving drunk. You know the state is cracking down on DUIs. He didn't have a choice. You were on Main Street, for crying out loud. Everyone knew you were drunk. Apparently you made quite a scene at El Rancherito too from what I heard."

"From who? Your stupid friend Maria?"

"One, don't call her that. And two, she said you slapped her butt and hit on her, like some jerk. Did you forget that you're a married man?"

"Hmph. I was just playin'. She should be flattered."

Soledad shook her head in disgust. "You can be so gross," she said.

Anger flared in Jorge's eyes and he rushed the bars. Soledad pushed back in fear, knocking the chair over behind her. He reached through the bars, just missing grabbing her jacket.

"Take it back," he ordered. "Or I swear..."

Soledad felt the familiar fear in her gut and nodded. "I'm sorry. I didn't mean it."

She heard the jangling of keys and the door opened. "Everything okay in here?" Brian asked.

"Fine, fine," she replied. "I just knocked the chair over accidentally."

Brian looked from Soledad to Jorge, who still stood up against the bars, and frowned. "Okay, I guess," he said as he shut the door.

"See what you did?" Jorge hissed.

Soledad ignored him and reset the chair, this time further back from the bars. "Have you eaten breakfast?" she asked.

"I'm not hungry."

"You're still drunk."

"So, what if I am?"

Soledad sighed. "Does Rosaria know where you are?"

"Not unless you told her."

"Why would I be asking then?"

Jorge took a step back and his lips curled in a thin smile.

"What is it?"

"I need you to do me a favor," he said.

"What?"

"I need you to go out to the house and check on Rosaria."

"Check on her? Why, what's wrong with her?"

"She's finally taking down the crib in the baby's room."

Soledad gasped. "She must be devastated."

"Hmph. I wouldn't know. I locked her in until she gets it done," he said smugly. He turned around and strolled back to the bench. He sat long ways with his feet on the bench and back against the wall. He crossed his fingers behind his head.

"You did what?" Soledad asked, shocked.

"You heard me. She should have done it a long time ago, so I made it happen."

"She's been in there all night?"

"Yeah. Well, not exactly. She's been there since Friday night." He laughed cruelly. "You should probably go check and see if she's done."

A thousand words ran through Soledad's head, but she stopped herself from saying them out loud. She was safe now, with bars between them. But she knew he would make her regret it when he got out if she spoke her mind. She went to the end of the corridor and banged on the door. After a few seconds had passed and Brian still hadn't opened the door, she banged again.

"Let me out," she yelled.

"I'm coming; I'm coming. Geez." He opened the door and she pushed past him.

"Everything okay?" Brian asked as she rushed to the front door.

"Fine," she replied brusquely.

# Chapter 17
## 1849

Rose felt great respect for the women who had babies along the trail and moved on the next day. She felt weak and exhausted from lack of sleep and limited diet. Little Joseph never let her sleep for more than a few hours at a time, and Paul, despite his best efforts, wasn't much of a cook.

The first few days before her milk came in had been the hardest. Joseph was hungry all of the time, and Rose felt so helpless trying to satiate his thirst.

She forced herself up every morning to fix breakfast and spent the days preparing to leave, hoping another wagon train would pass by in time.

"How much longer do we have, do you think?" Paul asked. He carried a bundle of sticks for the fire under his left arm and his crutch under the right. His leg was still too weak to hold his weight.

"The moon was close to full on the night Joseph was born, and the Apache were here a few nights before the new moon, which means we probably have a week and a half at most."

Paul frowned. "I think we have to face it. There aren't going to be any other wagon trains this season. It's too late."

"I was thinking about that," Rose replied. "Remember the family who were lodging in the old Pratt house? They were going to join our train, but didn't have the money. I remember her saying that she would catch the next one."

"She may have, but that doesn't mean it was going to be this season."

Rose sighed. "True. So, what are we going to do? I don't know the last time the horses have been ridden. They've been pulling wagons for as long as I can remember. And we only have one saddle."

"We don't have much of a choice. One of us will have to ride bareback."

"I guess so."

"And we need to start mounting and riding them a little bit each day to get them accustomed to having a rider."

"And if they buck, someone in your condition is going to be able to wrangle them?"

"Rose, we don't have much choice. We can't be here when the Apache return. They made that very clear."

"I know; I'm sorry. I'm just worried."

"It'll be fine," he promised with meager conviction.

Little Joseph squawked from his bed inside the cabin and Rose went inside to retrieve him. She bundled him in a blanket, wrapped two ends over her shoulders and had Paul help her tie it in back. After some experimentation, she had learned that she could keep him close to her chest while she worked with both of her hands free. As soon as he felt himself snuggled against his mother, he calmed down and fell back to sleep.

"I'm going to get some more water," Rose announced. "The horses' trough is getting empty, and we are going to need some for dinner." The horses' trough was just a natural depression in the rock face deep enough to hold a few gallons of water.

"Okay, take the rifle."

Rose picked up the bucket she used whenever she needed enough water for the horses and grabbed the rifle from where it sat next to the door. Ever since that night with the coyotes, she never left the immediate area around the cabin without it. Paul had also taken to wearing the pistol on his hip. He was so thin, he looked like a child strapping on his father's belt, but they both felt better having their weapons close at hand.

Rose carefully climbed the rock and approached the pool. The water level in the basin had been slowly and naturally falling as they used it, with no clue or explanation for how it had filled on the night of Joseph's birth. Rose had searched the entire area for a spring or other source that could be feeding the pool. The water was crystal clear, and she could see the bottom of the basin. There were no visible cracks in the rock or movement that would indicate flow.

She dipped the bucket into the pool and sat it on the ledge next to the edge. It was always cool in the little depression, and she relished the shade for a moment.

Rose thought about her conversation with Paul and decided to climb to the top of the ridge to look out over the valley. Maybe she would see someone off in the distance. She left the bucket there, but carried the rifle with her. Keeping it with her had become a habit.

The rockface appeared smooth from a distance, but was rough to the touch, like sandpaper against her skin. She found the familiar footholds and pulled herself up to the ridge. Thinking back to the first day when the wagon train had left them behind, she sat down with her feet dangling over the side. So much had happened in a few short weeks.

The sun was high in the sky and she held a hand over her eyes to block its glare. She flinched when a crack of gunfire suddenly echoed across the valley. She clenched the rifle tight and frantically searched the valley.

"Did you hear that?" she called out.

Paul hobbled into view and looked up at her. "Yes, was that a gunshot?"

"I think so," she replied.

"What do you see?"

"Nothing yet."

She scanned the valley again, this time focusing on the mountain pass where the trail dropped into the valley. A cloud of dust emerged from the pass, followed by the faint sound of pounding hooves.

"Horses," she reported. "Coming out of the pass."

"Stay up there," Paul ordered. "Out of sight until we know who they are."

"Be careful," she said.

"I will. Don't worry."

Rose swung her legs back and crawled behind the lip of the ledge. Worried she wouldn't be able to help Paul if he needed it, she scrambled down the rock face and carefully untied the blanket. She gently bundled it under the baby and rested him in a natural depression in the rock. He gurgled and smiled in his sleep, but didn't wake.

"Sshhh, little one. Stay asleep."

Rose climbed back to the top and lay on her belly. She found a toe hold to keep her in place on the slope and craned her neck to see over the rock.

# CHAPTER 18

## 2024

As she climbed higher, Rosaria stopped more frequently to rest. She shivered and struggled to catch her breath.

"I'm out of shape," she gasped. She unclipped the water bottle and took a drink. She shook the bottle, realizing it was almost gone. "I haven't even reached the top yet, and my water's almost gone. I should have topped it off in the creek."

She was following a narrow canyon up the slope, but the little stream had petered out hours back. Her hands hurt from the cuts and scrapes she incurred climbing over rocks and pushing through tree branches.

Her thighs burned from climbing, and she was certain she had blisters on both heels. Physically, she was miserable, but the pain couldn't stifle her new-found sense of freedom and independence.

The shadows grew longer, and she didn't want to be caught in the same position as the night before.

"I need to find shelter for the night and build a fire," she said.

The canyon seemed to end just in front of her, so she scrambled up the loose shale side to the top, causing the rocks to shift and tumble to the base. She grabbed onto a tree branch and pulled herself up over the lip. From that vantage point, she could follow her trail back down through the canyon. She marvelled at how far she'd come. She turned to look up at how far she had to go, but could only see pine trees and rocks, the same view she'd had all afternoon.

She began to look for a place to make camp and followed the base of a rocky ledge until it turned upwards. She rounded the corner and was surprised to find a cavern cut out of the rock face. She stepped inside to explore. The ground was littered with leaves, twigs, and pine needles. She saw no sign that the cavern was inhabited by animals or recently visited by humans.

She crouched low to avoid hitting her head on the low ceiling and made her way to the back of the cavern. It was completely silent and still. She sat down to take in her surroundings, staring up at the ceiling. It took her a moment to realize what she was looking at. A black spot in the ceiling stood out in stark contrast to the red-brown natural rock. A small hole in the rock was barely visible at the center of the smudge. She reached up to touch the area and then examined her finger—soot.

Although there were no signs of recent use, the cavern had clearly been used in the past. The soot was clear evidence of multiple fires, and she wondered how long it could have been there to still rub off on her finger.

When she looked back to the entrance of the cavern, she realized it wasn't completely natural. From the inside, she could see that rocks had been piled on each side to narrow the entrance. It would have helped to block the inhabitants from the elements and provide protection.

Rosaria silently thanked whoever had gone before and built the shelter. It was sheer luck that she had run into it.

She spent the next hour gathering branches and dry pine needles for her fire. She didn't know exactly what she was doing, so she formed a pile of needles and then placed small sticks on top of them. She kept the bigger branches off to the side.

She took the lighter from her backpack and held the flame to the needles. They smoldered, but quickly went out.

She tried over and over with the same result.

"What else could I use?" she asked, hoping the spirits of the previous occupants were listening. She sat back against the wall and tucked her hands in her pants pocket.

"Wait, what is this?" she asked. She pulled a piece of paper from her pocket and unfolded it on her knee. It was the original note she had written to Jorge.

"How appropriate," she said. She rolled the paper into a loose ball and stuffed it under the pile of needles. She lit the lighter and held the flame to the paper until it caught. The flame crackled and grew as a breeze rushed through the cabin, encircling Rosaria in a cool hug and feeding the fire. The needles caught and lapped at the twigs.

Soon, she had a warm fire burning and casting dancing shadows against the cavern walls. The smoke disappeared into the little hole at the center of the soot stain, a natural chimney in the rock. She fed the fire with the larger pieces of wood and went outside to gather enough to last her through the night. The flame reflected off of the cavern walls, warming the rocks. She didn't have much water left, but she was warm and comfortable, and that was enough for the moment.

*** 

Soledad raced up the gravel driveway, afraid of what she would find in the trailer. Without food, water, or a bathroom, Rosaria could be in an awful state. The two women weren't close (how could they ever be with Jorge between them?) but Soledad did her best to protect Rosaria by keeping Jorge happy.

He hadn't always been this way. When they were young, Jorge protected her from their foster father, often getting beaten in her place. She owed him for that. It wasn't until he was in high school and started drinking that his cruelty manifested itself.

It broke her heart. He had always sworn he would never treat anyone the way they had been treated, but the years of abuse had worn him down until he was no different than their foster dad. A part of him realized he had become the monster he had fought so hard against, and he loathed himself for it. Soledad was certain that was part of the reason Jorge drank so much, even though ironically, the drink made it worse. He never had a role model showing him there was a different way.

"Not that that excuses it," she said as she skidded to a stop in the yard and threw the car into park. "I can't believe he locked her in the room."

She jumped out and fumbled in her purse for the extra key to their trailer. She unlocked the door and knocked as she opened it and entered.

"Rosaria, it's Soledad. Are you okay?"

There was no response, and Soledad felt a lump form in her stomach.

"Rosaria, it's me. It's going to be okay."

She rushed down the hall to the nursery door and wriggled the knob. It turned easily in her hand, clearly unlocked. The door squeaked as she pushed it open and looked into the room only to find the crib still standing and the room empty.

She felt a rush of relief wash over her. "She got out, at least," she said. "Rosaria? Rosa? Where are you?"

Rosaria didn't drive and never left the house without Jorge or Soledad. Where could she be? Asleep? Soledad rushed into the master bedroom. The bed was unmade and the dresser drawers hung open, but Rosaria wasn't there. It only took a minute for Soledad to search the rest of the single wide trailer.

It wasn't until she opened the fridge to grab a bottle of water that she noticed the note hanging under the Albuquerque magnet. She pulled off the magnet and held the note to the light.

"That's weird," she said. "When was the last time her sister ever came over? I haven't seen her in years."

She read the note again. Something didn't sit right. "Your sister needed help? With what? She has a family and friends there. Why would she need you?"

She unscrewed the lid from the water and took a long drink while she pondered. She swallowed and wiped the edges of her mouth. "Maybe Rosaria finally left him." She nodded her support if that was indeed true. She thought about whether she should go back to the jail and tell Jorge.

"If the note is real, Rosaria will be back home tomorrow and at work before Jorge can be released. He'll never know the difference. But on the other hand, if she left him, that gives her another day's head start."

She thought some more, finally coming to a decision.

"Good for her," she finally said. "She deserves better." She crumpled up the note and stuffed it in her pocket. "Either she comes back or she doesn't. Frankly, I hope she left and that she makes it to wherever she's going."

Soledad walked through the house and flicked off the lights. She threw the bedcovers up over the mattress and closed the drawers. As she walked past the nursery door, on a whim she locked the door before pulling it shut.

As she climbed into her car, she felt butterflies in her stomach, nervous for Rosaria's sake. "Wherever you are girl, I'm with you. *Vaya con Dios*."

# CHAPTER 19

## 1849

R ose flinched involuntarily at the sound of gunshots echoing through the valley. As the riders got closer, she realized she was looking at two distinct dust clouds, one chasing the other. The pounding of hooves grew louder and she heard the riders shouting.

"I see two riders chasing a group of four, no five. They're shooting at each other." Rose had to shout over the sound of the galloping horses.

"Stay put," Paul ordered.

The first group barreled into the yard, rolling from their horses before they were at a full stop. Dust enveloped the camp site, blocking Rose's view. The men scattered, looking for cover while yelling at each other.

Rose watched as two of them raced into the cabin, and then cursed that it provided such poor cover. She heard the scraping of barrels against the ground as they moved them into position at the front wall.

The others scrambled to find cover elsewhere, but there were no rocks or trees big enough to hide behind, so two of them finally joined the others in the cabin. Rose strained her neck trying to see where the fifth was hiding, but couldn't see him anywhere.

There was a brief moment of silence where the chaos and confusion seemed to hang suspended in time. The riders' horses could smell the small amount of water in the little trough and pushed against the rope fence trying to get in, their flanks covered in sweat. The dust began to settle and the men grew quiet. Rose wondered where Paul was hiding. She had last seen him entering the cabin.

The brief moment of silence was shattered as the two men in chase pulled up short at the sight of the cabin. The horse in front whinnied and reared up on its hind legs.

"Woah, there," Rose heard the man say. He was wearing a navy blue wool shirt with yellow piping.

"Come out with your hands up," the man ordered, pointing his rifle at the cabin.

There was no response from the gang.

The rider shifted in his saddle and Rose got a better look. She recognized the man's dragoon uniform immediately and the distinct triple V designator on his sleeve. The men inside the cabin with her husband must be outlaws, deserters, or some other type of ne'er do wells. They couldn't be up to anything good if the army was chasing after them.

"You've got to the count of ten," the sergeant said. "You've got nowhere to run Bill. Your horse thievin' days are over."

The other soldier slid quietly from his horse and crouched low as he dove behind a small mound and took aim at the cabin. Rose flinched, knowing the mound was a red ant hill.

They seemed to be at a stalemate. Rose pushed herself a little further up on the rock to get a better view and examined the horses. They all carried the US brand.

As the sergeant continued to talk, he weaved back and forth on his horse in an irregular pattern so as not to create a static target. He kept his distance at a range that would be tough for even the best shot.

The private glanced over at his sergeant, and the sergeant gave a slight flick of the wrist. The private nodded and began making his way in a wide arc to the side of the cabin where the horses were still trying to get at the water. Rose remembered she had a full bucket sitting next to the basin to fill the trough. There definitely wasn't enough water for an extra five thirsty animals.

"We've got you red-handed Bill. Those horses belong to the United States Army, and I can see their brands from here. Your Mexican buyers are going to just have to be disappointed."

The private inched ever closer.

Suddenly, a shot rang out and the private grunted in pain and dove behind a creosote bush. From her vantage point, Rose could see him wince and grab his left shoulder. Blood seeped between his fingers.

The Sergeant reacted with lightning speed, bringing his Mississippi rifle to his shoulder and firing at the puff of smoke. A man screamed and Rose heard the thump of a body hitting the floor. One of the other bandits swore.

The sergeant busied himself reloading as he worriedly tried to assess his soldier's wounds. The private took his neckerchief from around his neck and, biting one corner, pulled it tight around the wound and tied it off.

The sergeant was clearly experienced. He had the percussion rifle reloaded by the time Rose glanced back and was aiming it at the cabin.

"You'll never take us alive, Sergeant Whitmer," one of the bandits yelled from inside the cabin.

"Suits me fine," Sgt. Whitmer replied. "Solves the problem of there bein' no hangin' trees in the area."

Rose immediately thought of the old piñon pine hidden behind the standing rock. She shuddered at the thought of it being used as a gallows.

As they talked, the private crawled on his belly toward the horses. Sgt. Whitmer glanced over and saw that he was moving again. As a distraction, Sgt. Whitmer moved his horse in the opposite direction and kept talking.

"That cabin isn't protecting anybody from a bullet. You know that."

"Your man's down and it's four to one. Them's good odds in my book."

"You'd need at least ten men for the odds to be even close to even," Sgt. Whitmer boasted, still trying to distract them. "Private Jones could take any two of you with his hands tied behind his back."

"Maybe if'n we hadn'a just shot him."

Quick as a snake, Sgt. Whitmer aimed in and fired off another shot. The bullet smashed through the wood wall and pinged off of something metal. The men in the cabin responded with a volley of pistol fire, but at that distance failed to hit anything. Sgt. Whitmer expertly controlled the horse as he reloaded once again.

Rose prayed that Paul was safely hidden and protected from the shots.

Under cover of gunfire, Pvt. Jones jumped to his feet and raced to the horses. Deciding it would be too difficult to guide them away, he untied the rope from the fence post and led the horses into the corral. They eagerly followed him inside, pushing at each other for access to the dregs at the bottom of the trough. Pvt. Jones refastened the corral rope and, using the horses as cover, began circling back to a position where he could help in the fight.

Rose held her father's old Hall rifle tightly in her hands, knowing she only had one shot if she had to use it. She heard Joseph gurgle in his sleep and silently prayed that he would remain asleep despite the ruckus of shouting and gunfire.

"Looks like a stand-off, then," the man called Bill yelled. "You're gonna spend a hot day out there in the sun."

# CHAPTER 20

## 2024

R osaria's eyes flew open, her heart racing. *What was that?* she thought. The fire had burned down to barely glowing embers and the cavern was pitch black in the night. She lay as still as possible, holding her breath for fear it would be too loud.

A twig snapped at the mouth of the cavern. She could feel the sweat beading on her forehead. Something hissed, and a low menacing growl sent shivers up Rosaria's spine.

She heard a voice off in the distance, and the growl stopped short. In a rush of wind, the creature silently ran away.

The footsteps and voices grew louder until it felt like they were on top of her, about to step on her at any moment. Pebbles fell over the side of the ledge, cascading at the entrance to the cavern.

"She's got to be up here somewhere," a man said.

"She couldn't have gone far," another agreed.

Rosaria's heart sank. Had Jorge and his friends already found her—tracked her through the mountains? She had hoped her note would have given her at least another day.

"Remember what he said," the first man continued. "She's desperate and dangerous, so don't hesitate. If you see her, just shoot. Up here this far, no one will ever know"

"Right. Hey, I think it's gettin' too dark to continue, and she'll see our flashlights if we keep going. What do you think?"

"You're right. This is as good a place as any. We'll camp here and pick up trackin' her in the morning."

Tears streamed down Rosaria's face. Just shoot? Was Jorge really capable of that? She thought back over their marriage and nodded her head, answering her own question. Of course he was.

She listened as the two men shuffled around, setting up camp. They finally stopped moving and Rosaria heard one of them start snoring lightly soon thereafter. She didn't dare move for fear they would hear her. Her hip bone ached where it pressed against the stone floor and she slowly shifted to ease the pressure. She felt a tickle in her nose and felt panic rising in her chest. She couldn't sneeze—not now. She wriggled her nose to try and force the sensation away, but it persisted as though her body was trying to betray her. Finally, she reached up and scratched until the feeling subsided. She whispered a prayer of thanks.

The night was cold and long as she forced herself to stay awake and tried to come up with some way out of the situation. As soon as the sun came up, the men would resume their search and find the cavern. She considered making a run for it while they slept, but discounted that option immediately. She was too petrified to move and too unfamiliar with the area to move silently in the dark. Her only hope was to pray they would move on without realizing she was lying directly below their camp.

Finally, she lost her battle with exhaustion and closed her eyes. Dawn was seeping into the cavern when she was once again startled awake at the sound of a stream of liquid splashing on the rocks at the mouth of the cavern. She rubbed the crust from her tear stained eyes and gagged at the sight.

The stream stopped and she heard his footsteps retreating from the edge. "Get up," he said.

The other man grunted. "I'm up," he replied.

"You pack up and I'll search for her trail."

Rosaria silently pushed herself to her knees and stuffed her meager posses-sions into the backpack so that she would be ready to run if she had too. She crawled around the cavern, searching for a weapon until she found a stone the size of a fist that had tumbled from the section of wall to the side of the entrance. With the stone held tightly in her hand, she sat down to wait, unable to think of what else she could do.

"Got it!" the first man shouted with obvious glee. The sound seemed to come from uphill, which didn't make sense.

I haven't been up that way yet, Rosaria thought. She pressed her back against the wall and leaned over to peek around the wall. She had a clear view up the hill. She held her breath when a man stepped into view.

He squatted down to study the ground, then brushed his finger over a rock and held it up to get a better look. He stood up and turned, holding his finger up to show his companion. "Look at this," he said.

Rosaria watched in horror as a giant cat crested the hill behind the man, its tawny fur blending closely with the earth. Dark red blood soaked its shoulder and it seemed to favor that side as it stalked towards the unsuspecting hunter. Rosaria felt the sudden urge to shout out and warn the man, but couldn't seem to open her mouth or even blink.

"You must have winged her," the man said. "There's a blood trail."

Rosaria didn't even register the relief at learning they hadn't been talking about her.

Just then, the man glanced down and noticed the cavern sitting directly under their camp. He must have thought that the cat could have hidden there overnight and pointed. "There's a cave," he shouted. I bet she's hiding in there, right below us."

The mountain lion crouched low, preparing to pounce.

"I'm going to check it out."

Rosaria gasped involuntarily, and her hand flew up to cover her mouth.

"Freeze!" the man above her shouted. "It's behind you!"

"Whaa...?" The man on the hill's eyes went wide and he began to turn.

With a snarl, the cat pounced.

Crack! The shot slapped the morning air and echoed down the canyon.

"Ayyye," the first man screamed.

The cat hit him in the chest, knocking him over and landing on top of him.

"Doug, are you okay?" the hunter above her cried. He stumbled and ran towards his friend, his rifle still aimed at the cat.

Doug groaned. "Get it off me; I can't breathe."

The cat lay still.

"Scott, come on. It's heavy. Get her off of me."

Scott stood over the scene, transfixed.

"Scott. Hello?"

"Oh, yeah. Sorry."

Scott prodded the mountain lion with his rifle. When it didn't move, he set down the rifle and leaned over to help free his friend from under her weight.

Rosaria sighed with relief.

# CHAPTER 21

## 1849

"You want a stand-off then? Fine. We can wait for the entire regiment to catch up and then we'll see what happens." He was bluffing of course, but Bill didn't know that.

Sgt. Whitmer dismounted his horse and led her a safe distance away from the cabin. He reached into his saddle bags and calmly went about packing and lighting his pipe while he kept an eye on the cabin.

"What's going on out there?" Bill finally asked, unable to contain his curiosity.

"Oh nothin'" Sgt. Whitmer responded. "Just gettin' ready to smoke you all out of that ramshackle excuse for a cabin."

"Smoke us?" Bill asked.

Rose could hear the tremor in his voice.

Pvt. Jones made his way back to Sgt. Whitmer, and they conversed quietly for a moment before he nodded and moved back to cover.

*Don't go back to the anthill*, Rose thought. He must have somehow heard her message because he bypassed the hill and dropped to the earth in a natural dip in the sand.

Rose saw movement out of the corner of her eye and turned to see what it was. It took her a moment to see the man cutting a wide circle behind the soldiers' position. His clothes were the color of the sand and blended so well that he was practically invisible unless he was moving. With a surprising amount of patience, he worked slowly and silently as the soldiers focused all of their attention on the house.

"What is this place anyway?" Sgt. Whitmer asked conversationally. "Anybody home?"

"How should I know?" Bill responded. "Must be from the last wagon train through here, but nobody's here."

Rose sighed in relief. Paul must have found a good place to hide but Rose couldn't imagine where. The room was so small and devoid of furniture.

Sgt. Whitmer puffed on his pipe as he studied the scene. He glanced up at the rock, staring directly at Rose's position. He frowned and she froze.

"Psst," he whispered.

Pvt. Jones turned to look at him.

Sgt. Whitmer made a wide circle with his hand and then pointed up to the top of the rock. Pvt. Jones nodded and moved out to follow his orders.

Rose turned her attention back out into the desert and the circling bandit. It took her a moment to find him and she gasped at how far he had managed to sneak as the others talked. He would reach Sgt. Whitmer within minutes and Pvt. Jones was now out of range to help him.

Rose ducked back down and stared up at the sky. "What do I do? What do I do?" she whispered. *I can't let the bandits find me, but I can't let him kill the soldier either.*

Joseph wriggled in his blankets and opened his eyes, ready for his next meal.

Rose flipped back over to watch the scene unfold, still undecided at what to do. The bandit was creeping closer with each step. Sgt. Whitmer's horse whinnied, and he absently reached a hand back to comfort her, unaware she was warning him of danger.

"Turn around. Turn around," Rose whispered, but he didn't seem to hear her.

"I'll bet that place would go up in flames in seconds," Sgt. Whitmer said. He turned his pipe to empty the contents then tapped it against his boot. He stamped on the coals, twisting them into the dirt. He raised his right breast pocket flap and tucked the pipe inside.

Rose saw him glance to the side in the direction of the entrance to the crevice and nod slightly. She felt the urge to go back and protect her baby from the approaching soldier, but couldn't seem to tear herself away from the drama unfolding below her.

The horse thief slowly raised his arm, pistol in hand.

"You ever been stuck in a building on fire before, Bill? It ain't fun. Believe me."

"You wouldn't," Bill replied.

"Why not? It's either that or hang you."

The thief's finger closed on the trigger.

Joseph wailed.

"What the...?" Rose heard behind her.

Both Sgt. Whitmer and the horse thief looked up towards the sound. Everything seemed to happen at once.

Rose rested the rifle on the rock and closed her left eye. Carefully, she squeezed the trigger.

The horse thief looked down at his chest in surprise. Blood colored his shirt front.

Sgt. Whitmer instinctively dove to the side, unholstering his pistol as he rolled and jumped to his feet.

The rifle shot triggered an immediate response and the three remaining horse thieves opened fire into the desert, scattering their fire without pausing to aim.

An errant bullet grazed one of the horses and it panicked. The others fed off its fear and stampeded. They broke through the corral rope, tearing the posts completely up from the ground and dragging them along until the rope fell away under their hooves. Caught in the middle of the herd, the Callandish's team ran wild with fear, following the army mounts into the desert.

Sgt. Whitmer's training kicked in, and he charged the house, bobbing and weaving as he went. He grunted as a bullet struck him in the thigh and he tumbled forward. Undeterred, he caught himself and he pushed himself back up to his feet to continue his charge, firing at each muzzle flash until his own pistol was empty. When it clicked on an empty chamber, he recognized the sound immediately and he tossed it to the side. Another round punched him in the shoulder, knocking him sideways.

Without a reload, Rose slid down the rock face to get to Joseph, who's crying had reached a fever pitch. She reached the bottom and turned around.

Sgt. Whitmer reached the doorway. He managed to pull his bowie knife from its scabbard and held it at the ready in his remaining good hand. His trouser leg was soaked with blood and sweat poured down his forehead. His right arm hung limply at his side. As his eyes adjusted to the sudden shadows in the cabin, he saw the shadow of a gun butt an instant before it struck him hard in the temple.

Another shot rang out, and then all went quiet.

Rose's hands trembled and her breath caught in her chest. Pvt. Jones stood in front of her cradling little Joseph in his arms. He looked Rose up and down and leered, showing a mouth full of stained and rotten teeth.

"Why hello, little lady," Pvt. Jones said, his voice high and reedy. He stared at her chest and licked his lips.

Joseph continued to cry in confusion, hunger, and anger at the unfamiliar man keeping him from his mother.

Rose's body responded to the crying, her milk leaking through her dress.

Pvt. Jones lifted his eyebrows in confusion at the spreading milk stains.

"Please," Rose said. "Give him to me." She took a tentative step forward, reaching out to take the baby.

Pvt. Jones stepped back, twisting the baby away from her. "After," he said. "My turn first."

"Please," she begged. "He's hungry."

"So am I."

"Rose? Rose, are you okay? What about the baby?" Paul called from the base of the rock.

Pvt. Jones' glare broke away from her chest and he looked at her in surprise. He had assumed she was alone.

"My husband," Rose said resolutely. "Give me the baby."

Pvt. Jones held a finger to his lips. "Sshhh," he said.

"Rose?" Paul called out again.

# CHAPTER 22

## 2024

The two hunters took their time cleaning and dressing the mountain lion. Scott couldn't resist reminding Doug over and over about how he'd saved his life.

"Yeah, Scott, for the thousandth time, it was a great shot. You saved my life. Now, can we get on with it?"

"In mid-air man. One more second, and his teeth would have been around your neck. Ha. What a shot. I've never seen anything like it."

"If you don't say so yourself."

"Hey, I saved your life, man."

"I know. You've already said that. Come on, help me with its hind leg here." Doug grimaced and put a hand to his shoulder. At first he thought it was just a bruise from where the heavy animal had landed on him, but when he checked, he was surprised to find ugly red claw marks running down his shoulder. The bleeding was minimal and the wounds weren't deep, but he caught the whiff of putrid meat everytime he turned his head in that direction.

"What is it?" Scott asked.

"Its claws got me in the shoulder," Doug said. "But not deep."

"We gotta get that cleaned out. Their claws carry all sorts of germs and stuff."

"Do you have your first aid kit?"

"Uhm." Scott thought about it for a second. "No, I think I left it down in the truck."

"So then, let's hurry all right?"

The two men worked together silently as Rosaria watched. Her stomach grumbled and her throat felt like dry cotton.

*Maybe I should go out and ask them for help,* she thought, but immediately dismissed the idea. She thought she recognized Scott from the store, and if he was from town, he'd know Jorge. It wasn't worth the risk.

Cleaning and preparing the animal took the men much longer than she thought and the sun was high in the sky before they finally stood up and wiped their knives on their blood stained pant legs.

Doug climbed back to their camp to grab their gear while Scott waited. They secured the cat's hide to Doug's pack and Scott led off down the trail. The coppery scent of blood was heavy on the air, and flies buzzed around the pile of meat and offal the men left behind.

"Hope we don't run into the warden," Doug said as they passed the cavern. He glanced over at the dark opening and Rosaria ducked quickly out of sight. "We should check that cave out."

"No time," Scott responded. "These scratches are already starting to burn. We need to get back."

Rosaria waited for what seemed like an hour after the men left. A crow cawed and landed on the cat's remains, happily thanking the men for such a grand meal. Eventually Rosaria crawled out of the cave. Her shoulders were stiff and back sore from sitting so still on the cold stone for so long. She rolled her neck and shoulders and reached down to touch her toes.

She contemplated popping an ibuprofen, but didn't know that she would be able to swallow it dry. She climbed the slope to the ledge over the cave and examined the men's campsite. A protein bar wrapper lay next to a mostly empty bottle of water.

Rosaria rushed to the bottle and fell to her knees. She unscrewed the cap and held it to her mouth, relishing the single sip as it washed over her dry throat. She held the bottle higher and shook it until the last drop landed on her tongue. The little taste of water felt so good, but seemed to magnify her thirst, leaving her wondering if she would have been better off not finding it at all.

***

"I am fining you $500 and sentencing you to 24 hours of community service, Mr. Campos. You can pay the cashier downstairs. The DMV will also be revoking your license for one year."

"What the...?" Jorge began.

"I wouldn't finish that sentence if I were you, Mr. Castro," the judge said, holding up his index finger in warning.

"How am I supposed to get to work?"

"Your Honor," the judge prompted.

"How am I supposed to get to work, your Honor?" Jorge repeated.

"That's not my problem, Mr. Castro. You should have thought about that before you got behind the wheel drunk."

"I don't have $500," Jorge protested.

The judge sighed. "Bailiff, will you please escort Mr. Castro out before I choose to make him a long term guest of the county?"

The bailiff nodded and approached Jorge. Jorge began to protest, but the bailiff whispered for him to shut his mouth as they walked out of the courtroom. "That was dumb," the bailiff said. "He could have given you ninety days in jail." The bailiff unlocked Jorge's handcuffs and attached them to a strap on his belt.

Jorge rubbed his wrists. "Where do I go?" he asked.

"Downstairs and to the right. Go up to the window and tell her your name. Then you can go over to the jail and retrieve your belongings."

Jorge waited in line at the window as a woman he recognized as the wife of one of his co-workers spoke quietly with the cashier. When she turned around, Jorge saw that she was crying. He looked away uncomfortably, hoping she wouldn't look at him.

"Next," the clerk said.

Jorge stepped forward and gave her his name. She looked him up on the computer and waited for a piece of paper to emerge from the printer.

"You have two weeks to pay your fine. Here is a list of places where you can finish your service hours. You will need to give them this piece of paper and have them sign off on your hours. Service hours must be completed within 90 days. Do you have any questions?"

Jorge took the piece of paper and tried to make sense of it. He felt overwhelmed with so much information.

"What if I don't have the $500?"

"If you don't pay in the allotted time, a warrant for your arrest will be entered into the system and you will be required to serve your time in county lockup."

"I can barely pay my bills as it is," Jorge argued.

The clerk glanced up for the first time, bored from a conversation she clearly had multiple times a day. "The court is not responsible for how you come up with the money. You are free to look into loans or other options, but we cannot advise you. Now, will that be all?"

Jorge hastily folded the piece of paper and stuffed it into his back pocket. He stormed out of the courthouse and walked to the police station next door. The officer at the front desk was ready with his personal possessions and made him sign a form before handing him the bag.

Jorge dumped the contents of the bag on the desk containing his wallet, phone, keys, and a used tissue. He left the dirty tissue on the counter and tried to turn on the phone. It was completely dead.

"Can I use your phone?" Jorge asked. "My phone's dead, and I apparently have to get a ride."

"There's a payphone over there," the officer said, pointing to an ancient looking phone on the wall.

"Payphone?"

The officer nodded.

Jorge sighed and shook his head. He found a quarter tucked into the corner of the wallet's cash pocket. He dropped the coin in the machine and dialed his work.

"Hey, it's Jorge. Is the boss there?"

"You're late—again," Thalia, the receptionist said.

"Yes, thank you Thalia. I would have never known. Just get me the boss, okay?"

Thalia grunted and set the phone down on the desk harder than necessary. Jorge held the receiver away from his ear.

The boss picked up the phone. "Out of jail, are you?"

Jorge groaned. Of course he knew. In this dump of a town, probably everyone knew. "Just a misunderstanding," Jorge said.

"What, you misunderstood that you had too much to drink?"

"Look, boss. I just need a ride home to get changed and then I can come into work. I'll make up the hours, I swear."

"Come into work and do what, Jorge? You're a machine operator without a license. What is it you think you're going to do?"

"I can still drive the backhoe. That's not on the street."

"No license, no job. Sorry Jorge, but you knew that when you got hired."

"Come on man. I need the money to pay my court fine. I'll do whatever you need. I'll take out the trash. I'll clean the freakin' trucks."

The boss thought about it for a minute. "You really put me in a bind, Jorge. We're on a deadline and now I don't have my backhoe operator. I'm not inclined to help you out after you screwed me over."

"Come on. I didn't do it to you. It's the stupid judge."

The boss sighed. "Fine. You can clean the trucks and the shop, but that job only pays minimum wage."

"What? That's not fair."

"Would you rather work with your wife at the dollar store?"

Jorge paused his tirade. "Fine. Just send Jimbo out to pick me up, will ya?"

"Straight home and back to work," the boss said.

"Whatever," Jorge said as he slammed the receiver down.

"Hey, careful with that," the officer shouted.

Jorge ignored him and stormed out of the station to wait for his ride.

# CHAPTER 23
## 1849

A million thoughts rushed through Rose's mind as she calculated options and odds. With the baby in Pvt. Jones' arms, she was limited in what she could do. She couldn't chance him dropping the baby.

She swallowed and forced herself to use her sweetest voice. "I'll do whatever you need me too, Private. But I need to feed the baby first, okay? What fun will it be if the baby is crying the whole time?" She felt bile rising her throat, disgusted by what she was forced to say.

Pvt. Jones looked suspiciously at her and then back at the crevice.

"He has a bum leg," Rose explained. "He can't come up here. So, just let me tell him everything is fine, and then I'll feed the baby quickly and, well, then we can..." She forced herself to wink and smile coyly. It felt so unnatural to her, but Pvt. Jones didn't seem to notice.

He licked his lips at the prospect.

She reached out for the baby, but Pvt. Jones didn't budge. "How do I know you ain't foolin' me?"

"Because you're young and strong and my husband's lame and weak. Any woman would take you over that."

He seemed to be processing her explanation. Finally he nodded and held out the baby. She rushed forward and took Joseph in her arms, noticing the blood still soaking through the dirty neckerchief tied around Pvt. Jones' arm.

"Tell him," he ordered.

Rose nodded. "We're fine, Paul," she called out. "I was just trying to calm little Thomas. Are you okay?"

*Little Thomas?* Paul thought from down below. *What does that mean?* "The Army sergeant is knocked out cold and bleeding pretty bad," he said. He thought for another second. *Is she trying to tell me she's still in danger?* "I'm just gonna get out your sewing kit and see if I can close the wound."

Rose smiled. *He doesn't know how to suture. He must understand I'm trying to tell him something,* Rose thought excitedly. "That's fine, darling. I'm just going to feed Thomas and then we'll be down shortly. Remember what Eliza taught us on the trail about treating injuries."

Pvt. Jones looked at Rose suspiciously. "That's enough," he said. "Feed the kid."

Paul's heart sank as he understood the message. Eliza hadn't taught him how to suture. But she had told them a harrowing story about her mom being attacked by the mine owner's son back in Scotland, which had motivated her to escape the mines and earn enough money for a boat to America. He looked down at the wounded sergeant. "I'm sorry," he whispered. "I have to go to my wife."

Sgt. Whitmer's eyes fluttered open and he groaned.

"I'll be right back," Paul said. "My wife's in danger."

Sgt. Whitmer blinked and wrinkled his forehead in confusion. Who was this man?

"It's a long story," Paul said. "The horse thieves are all dead here, but someone is up there with my wife." Paul pointed up at the rock.

Realization hit Sgt. Whitmer, and he struggled to sit up. He had sent Pvt. Jones up to the top of the rock before the shooting started—the same Pvt. Jones who had been court-martialed for that incident in Mexico. And now he was alone with a woman.

"No, you're hurt." Paul placed a hand on Sgt. Whitmer's shoulder.

Sgt. Whitmer cleared his throat and tried to talk. It still came out with a croak. "It's my fault," he said. He swallowed and coughed.

"What's your fault?"

"I sent Jones up there." It hurt to breathe, but he pushed through the pain. "Gun?" he asked.

Paul rushed inside and brought out his pistol and a handful of rounds. He hastily reloaded the gun while Sgt. Whitmer tied a tourniquet around his upper thigh.

Whitmer subconsciously registered that he had lost way too much blood. He wanted nothing more than to lie down and sleep, even if for just a moment, but he forced himself to stand.

Paul handed him the loaded gun,

"Show me the way," Sgt. Whitmer ordered.

The two made quite a pair, with one hobbling on a crutch and the other limping on his bad leg, but they were both determined to make it in time. Sgt. Whitmer entered the crevice first and climbed by sheer force of will, using every ounce of strength left in his body.

*I will not leave this world with her in Jones' grubby hands. If it's the last thing I do.*

"So, what's your name, Private?" Rose asked as she slipped her blouse down and the baby latched onto her breast. She forced herself to hide her disgust as the grimy man ogled her body.

"Jed," he replied absently, his anticipation growing.

"Where are you from, Jed?" Rose asked, determined to keep him distracted. "How long have you been in the Army?"

*Please Paul. Please do something.*

"I'm from Arkansas. Joined up at the beginning of the Mexican War."

"You must be so brave. I'll bet you're up for promotion soon."

He looked away and scowled.

She sighed at the brief respite from his gaze.

"I was a Corporal," he said. "Busted down for doin' what any other man would do given the chance."

Rose could see his anger growing and tried to diffuse the situation.

"That is so unfair. I'm sure that you did nothing wrong. You seem like such a good soldier."

"Shouldn'a let her go," he mumbled. "She wouldn't have been able to tell the lieutenant."

Rose shivered. She could feel evil emanating from him, barely disguised behind the respectability of the uniform. She would have to play this very carefully.

"Tell me about your family back home," she prodded. The baby stopped drinking and she held him against her shoulder to burp. She patted his back as she struggled to come up with a plan.

"Done?" Jed asked eagerly.

"Not quite. He needs to burp and then feed on the other side."

"He can have the rest later," Jed decided. "Put him down."

Rose held the baby closer, wrapping her arms protectively around him. "He'll just start crying again if I don't let him finish," she implored.

"I don't care," he said coldly. Jed unbuttoned his uniform blouse and tried to take it off, but struggled to pull it down over his injured arm. He winced in pain and swore.

"That looks painful," Rose said. "Maybe you should let me take a look at it. We could go down and have my husband sew it up."

He scowled.

*It was worth a try*, she thought.

He pulled the blouse back up over his shoulders and began to fumble with the buttons of his trousers.

"I don't want you to get hurt," Rose said, pointing at his arm. "I swear. We can take care of your arm and then do whatever you want."

"You think I'm stupid?" he hissed. "Now lay down and shut up. No more talkin'."

"Okay, okay." She took her time laying the baby back in the little depression, carefully wrapping him in the blanket.

Suddenly, hands grabbed her shoulders from behind and forced her around. He pushed her to the ground, and she banged her head against the rock. She saw stars for a moment and bucked under his weight. He grabbed her wrists, pinning them to the ground next to her head. He grinned and she gagged at his hot foul breath. He forced both wrists above her head and held tight with his good hand while his other fumbled clumsily, pawing over her body.

She twisted and writhed, but he just laughed.

"Give me a good fight, girly," he whispered in her ear, glee evident in his voice. He grabbed her skirts and adjusted his weight so that he could pull them up.

Tears stung her eyes. She couldn't move under his weight and strength, even with his injured arm. She turned her head to the side to try and escape his breath and saw movement through her tears.

"Get off of her," a weak voice commanded.

Jed ignored the command and redoubled his efforts to pull up her skirts.

"I said, get off," the voice said, stronger this time.

Suddenly, Jed yelped and Rose felt his weight leave her body. She opened her eyes but couldn't understand what she was seeing. The sergeant stood above her holding Jed by the scruff of his neck, but he looked like a ghost. Jed vainly struggled to free himself from the specter.

In a voice like ice, the sergeant spoke. "Private Jedediah Jones, I sentence you to death for your crimes committed here today. They should have done it the last time."

"Sarge, no. You don't understand. She wanted..."

Crack!

The gunshot stopped him short, unwilling to hear his lies. The sergeant released his grip, and Pvt. Jones slumped to the ground. Rose scooted back onto her elbows and looked over in surprise to see Paul emerging from the crevice, anxiety written all over his face.

"I'm okay," Rose gasped. "It's over."

"Thank God," Paul replied.

Sgt. Whitmer's shadow fell over her, blocking the sun from her eyes. She turned back from Paul to thank him. "Thank you, Sergeant..." she began.

Sgt. Whitmer's eyes rolled back until all she could see was white. Rose registered that he looked a sickly shade of green as his knees gave way and he collapsed to the ground.

She crawled over to him and held his face in her hands. "Sergeant, wake up. Sergeant, can you hear me?"

He didn't respond.

She bent over, placing her ear against his lips. They felt cold. Tears clouded her vision and she began to shake. Paul took her in his arms and she buried her head in his chest.

"It's okay," he said, rocking her gently. "We're all okay."

# CHAPTER 24

## 2024

Jorge stomped into the trailer, his blood boiling at the injustice of it all. Losing his license, getting demoted—it was too much to take. If that sorry excuse for a wife had cleaned up the nursery when he told her to, none of this would have happened.

He pulled his belt off and stormed down the hall. He rattled the doorknob while shouting incoherently. He was so mad at her that he was shaking, and it took multiple tries to turn the little lock and open the door. He entered the room with the belt held over his shoulder, ready to strike. But the room was empty.

He barged through the rest of the house, yelling for Rosaria to show herself and take her beating. Finally, Jimbo walked inside to see what all of the ruckus was about.

"Where's my wife?" Jorge demanded.

Jimbo looked down at his watch. "Probably at work, which is where we need to be going."

Jorge let his arm drop when he realized Jimbo was probably right. But his desire to punish Rosaria remained unsatiated.

"Go shower and change," Jimbo said as he checked the fridge. He pulled out a can of beer and popped the top.

"Give me one of those," Jorge demanded.

Jimbo tossed him a can, and Jorge headed back to the shower.

Jimbo was working on a bag of pretzels when Jorge emerged in his work clothes. He plugged his dead phone into the charger on the counter and then signaled for Jimbo that it was time to go. Jimbo dropped the bag of pretzels on the couch and followed Jorge outside.

"Take me past the dollar store," Jorge said as Jimbo turned his truck around.

"We gotta get back to work. The boss said to bring you directly there."

"I haven't seen my wife all weekend. I just wanna say hi. It'll only take a second."

"Whatever," Jimbo replied and belched.

Jorge jumped out of the truck before Jimbo had a chance to throw the gear shift into park and barreled into the store. He saw Melanie at the checkout, lazily browsing through a magazine. Melanie looked up.

"Hey Jorge," she said. She placed the magazine down.

"Where's Rosaria?" Jorge asked.

Melanie frowned. "I was gonna ask you the same thing. Her shift started at ten and she never showed and didn't call."

Jorge was searching the aisles, but stopped suddenly when Melanie's words registered. "What do you mean she didn't show up?" he asked.

"I mean she didn't show up. What do you think I mean? Don't you know where your own wife is?"

Jorge lashed out, sweeping his arm across a shelf full of cups. Glass shattered across the floor.

"Hey, watch it," Melanie shouted.

"Tell her to call me if she shows up. Or else." He rushed to the door.

"You gotta pay for that," Melanie protested until she saw the look in Jorge's eyes. "Nevermind," she said. "Just go."

"Tell her," he repeated.

"Right. I will."

Jorge climbed into the cab. "Give me your phone," he demanded.

"What's wrong?" Jimbo asked.

Jorge snatched the phone from Jimbo's hand. "You have Soledad's number in here?" He scrolled through the contacts.

"Yeah," Jimbo replied. "What did Rosaria say?"

Jorge punched the call button. "She's not there."

"What?"

"Where's Rosaria?" Jorge demanded as soon as Soledad answered.

"Hello to you too," she said. "I see you've had your hearing."

"Where's my wife?" he screamed.

"What the hell, Jorge. Calm down."

"Answer my question."

"I don't know."

"How don't you know? Didn't you take her to work this morning?"

*That answers that question*, Soledad thought.

"No, I didn't," she replied.

"And why not?"

"When I went over the other day, there was a note that her sister needed her and would bring her back in time for work this morning."

"And you didn't think to tell me?"

"You were in jail, remember? And you locked her in a room for two nights and a day. So, I didn't really feel like talking to you again."

"Get over to the house, right now."

"I'm at work."

"I'm not asking."

"Screw you, Jorge," she yelled and hung up the phone.

Jorge threw the phone onto the dash.

"Hey, watch it. That's my phone," Jimbo protested. He leaned over and took his phone back.

"Take me home," Jorge demanded.

"The boss said to bring you straight to work."

"My wife is gone," Jorge said. "Do you think I really care about some stupid minimum wage cleaning job right now, Jimbo? Just take me home. Now."

Jimbo held up his hands in surrender. "All right. All right. But I'm not covering for you at work."

He pulled out of the lot and turned down Main St.

"Stop!" Jorge cried as they passed his truck, which still sat on the side of the road. Jorge opened the door. "Go to work," he said as he climbed out.

"But you can't drive."

"Thanks for the lift," Jorge said. He climbed into his truck and turned the key. The engine roared to life.

Jimbo shook his head. "It's your life, man," he said as he whipped his truck around and headed back to work.

# Chapter 25
## 1849

Rose broke away from Paul's embrace and crawled on hands and knees to the edge of the pool. She dunked her head into the water and screamed. Bubbles carried the sound to the surface. She felt Paul's hand on her back and jerked her head out of the water, gasping for breath. She began scrubbing her wrists where Jed had held them, then continued to scrub every place he had touched.

In a frenzy, she tore off the clothes he had manhandled and dunked them into the pool. She scrubbed the fabric against the side of the pool, desperate to cleanse it of his filth.

Paul watched in horror, unsure what to say or do. Finally, Rose collapsed to the ground, her chest heaving. Paul slipped out of his jacket and gently covered her. He barely noticed that the basin had emptied itself somehow when he reached in to grab her wet clothes. Not knowing what else to do, he gently laid out the clothes on the rock to dry.

Joseph began to cry and Paul scooped him up into his arms. "You're okay, sweet baby." He leaned down and kissed him on the forehead.

"He needs to finish eating," Rose said.

Paul looked over and saw that she was sitting up with his jacket wrapped around her shoulders. He handed her the baby and then wrapped them both in the blanket.

"You scared me," he said

She leaned in, pressing her forehead against his.

"I'm okay now," she said

"Are you sure?"

"Yes, I'm sure." She looked over at the bodies of the two soldiers. What are we going to do about them?"

We don't want to leave them up here," he replied. They might contaminate the water. He looked over at the basin. Cool, clear water lapped at the edges, filled to the brim.

Rose sighed. "Let's get you down first. Then I can drag the bodies down."

"I can help," he protested weakly.

"Not yet. But soon. You'll be better soon." She got to her feet and grabbed Paul's crutch from where it leaned against a rock. She handed it to him and saw the bucket still sitting next to the basin. "I need to bring this down for the horses too."

Paul coughed and frowned.

"What?" she asked.

"There are no horses," he said. "They joined the stampede. They're long gone."

"Oh, yes. I forgot."

"No horses, no wagon, and just over a week to be gone from here."

They stood together without speaking, the only sound that of the baby hungrily eating.

Rose looked into Paul's eyes and saw the absolute absurdity of their situation. She began to laugh. Joseph stopped eating and looked up at her curiously. "This is worse than a Dickens novel," she said. Paul broke into laughter as well. Tears streamed down their faces as laughter echoed off the walls of the standing rock. Rose gasped for air and started laughing anew.

"What else could go wrong?" she asked.

"Do you want to find out? Because I'm sure we could think of something!"

They broke into laughter again until their bellies hurt.

"Let me have it, God. Do your worst," Rose said.

"Ask and ye shall receive," Paul joked.

# CHAPTER 26
## 2024

The hunters had forced a late start, so Rosaria pushed on with determination to make it over the crest of the mountain before dark. The going was steep and rocky, and she found herself tripping more than once. Her palms bled from scrapes, and her knees were covered in bruises, but she refused to stop.

At every step, she felt Jorge closing in on her, catching up. Her tongue felt swollen and her mind was foggy. She lost track of her surroundings and focused solely on keeping her feet moving.

Exhausted, hungry, and desperate for water, her mind started to wander. She thought back to happier days in a feeble attempt to motivate herself to believe she could be happy once again if she just took the next step and the one after that.

*It was the spring of her junior year in high school and she sat at a picnic table in the school courtyard talking excitedly with her best friend about who was going to ask them to prom. She had a huge crush on a boy in her history class and had managed to get herself into his group for their group presentation on the first Battle of Bull Run. They were meeting at his house after school to plan out their presentation.*

*"How did you manage it?" her friend Lupe asked, leaning in*

*conspiratorially.*

*"Mr. Oglethorpe was assigning groups because he doesn't believe in letting us choose, right?"*

*"Yeah, and?"*

*"Well, I've been paying attention during the year and figured out his system." Rosaria explained proudly.*

*Lupe's eyes grew wide in admiration. She and Rosaria had been best friends since the fifth grade, but Rosaria had always been the smart one. She got good grades and never struggled with her homework. Lupe would have failed multiple classes if it hadn't been for Rosaria's help. Rosaria never complained or put Lupe down. She just tutored her like it was the most natural thing for a friend to do.*

*"Well?" Lupe prodded.*

*Rosaria was staring across the courtyard where Francisco and his friends were casually passing a soccer ball back and forth.*

*"Earth to Rosaria," Lupe said, tugging on Rosaria's jacket sleeve.*

*"Huh?" Rosaria asked.*

*Lupe giggled. "You are so gone."*

*"Am not."*

*"Yeah, whatever. So, tell me. What is Mr. Oglethorpe's system?"*

*"Oh yeah, sorry. So, he always mixes the boys and girls when he makes groups right? I figured out that he just counts them out in class. Like, he will count the girls first, one through four, over and over. Then he does the boys. He puts together all of the ones, all of the twos, threes, and fours into their groups, and that's it."*

*"So, how did you beat that?*

*"Well, I knew he was going to be picking groups today, so I waited for Francisco to sit down, figured out his number, then found a seat that would end up being the same number."*

*"What if there wasn't a free seat where you needed it?"*

*Rosaria laughed. "Actually, there wasn't. I had to convince Sam to trade me seats. I told him I forgot my glasses and couldn't see the board properly."*

*"But you don't wear glasses."*

*"Don't tell Sam that!"*

*The two girls giggled and talked through the rest of lunch.*

"Ow!" Rosaria grunted, the pain bringing her back to the present. She pushed to her feet and looked down at her knees to assess the wound. There was a tear in her pants and her knee was bleeding.

She shrugged out of her backpack and set it on a rock. She rummaged through the pack until she found a bandage. She fiddled with the uncooperative wrapper until she managed to free the bandage and stick it to her skin. She stuffed the garbage back into her pack and sighed. It felt like she had been hiking for weeks, not just a couple of days.

"What day is it anyway?" she wondered. She thought back, biting her lower lip. "I left on Saturday and slept behind the cell tower building that night. So last night in the cave was Sunday night and the hunters were this morning. Was that just this morning? Geez, it seems like forever ago. So anyway, it's Monday afternoon." She looked up and realized the area was growing dark. "Monday evening rather," she said, correcting herself.

She took in her surroundings, the first time she had really done so for hours. The vegetation had thinned out some, but tall ponderosa pines still blocked her view of the valley below. She turned to look up and was surprised to find she was much closer to the top of the mountain than she had imagined. She must have walked further than she had thought.

Reinvigorated by the sight, she swung her backpack back over her shoulders and hiked with a newfound energy, her eyes focused on the top. As she crested the top, a gust of wind hit her square in the shoulders and she teetered on her back leg in surprise. She managed to shift her weight and find her balance as she turned around to gaze at the valley below. She could see a tiny speck of light where the trailer should be and a cluster of lights further along, which she guessed would be downtown.

"Strange," she said to the wind. "Now that I can look back and see how far I've come, all of the canyons, steep hills, briars, and the rest of it don't seem quite so bad."

The wind whistled around her in response. "If I could have only watched myself from up here, knowing I would make it." She felt something stir within her, a deep feeling of contemplation and peace. For so long she had battled through each day to just survive. It had been ages since she had really taken the time to think and evaluate what she truly wanted in life. How could she have when Jorge dictated her every decision?

"Is this what God sees?" she whispered. "Does He watch us, urging us to break free and begin our journey? Does He cheer us on as we climb our mountain?"

She turned around and stared out over the next valley to the west. The sun was setting on the horizon, painting the sky in blazing shades of red and purple. She looked down the mountain trying to pick out the easiest trail down, but the details were hidden in shadow.

"You're not some sort of philosopher," she told herself. "And you still have a long way to go." She chuckled. She had always been prone to daydream, but that was a long time ago.

She thought about finding a place to camp for the night, but decided she had lost enough time that morning hiding in the cavern. She pulled the flashlight from her backpack and stuck it in her back pocket, ready to use as soon as it grew too dark to see. She needed to press forward.

***

When Jorge got back to the house, his phone had only charged to 53%, but he pulled it free and scrolled through his contacts for Rosaria's sister, Alejandra. He punched the call icon and waited. The phone rang three times and then stopped.

"Come on," he yelled and called again. This time it only rang once before disconnecting.

He clicked the messaging icon and typed out a quick text:

> Answer the phone. It's about Rosaria.

> I'm at work.

> Is she there with you?
> ⌷⌷⌷⌷

> ??

> I can't find her.

His phone rang seconds later.

"What do you mean, you can't find her? She's not your car keys that you can just misplace. What did you do?"

Jorge held the phone away from his ear until she finished. He had been the one prepared to yell at her. "I didn't do anything," he said when she finally gave him a chance to speak. "I was in jail..."

"For hurting her? I knew it—that one day, you would go too far. You piece of utter..."

"Shut up!" Jorge yelled, unable to take it any longer.

Alejandra stopped mid-sentence.

"Thank you. Geez, you're annoying."

"That's it. You can go...."

"Stop. Just listen for once. I got hit with DUI and couldn't get out until this morning when the judge came in, all right? I didn't do anything to her." His mind flashed on her face as she begged him not to lock her in the room. "She was fine," he lied. "When I got out this morning, she wasn't at work and she's not at home. Soledad said she left a note saying you needed her and picked her up."

"Me?"

"Yeah, you. So, did you?"

"Did I what?"

"Did you pick her up?"

"No. I was in Amarillo all weekend for a horse auction with my husband. I haven't talked to Rosaria for weeks. You won't let her."

"Hmmph," Jorge responded at the dig. "So where would she go?"

"Maybe she left your ass," Alejandra said, trying to hide the worry in her voice. "It's about time, too."

"Just shut up," Jorge said. "Look, just call me if you hear from her, okay?"

"Fat chance," Alejandra responded and ended the call.

"Is everything all right?" Alejandra's coworker Penny asked.

"I don't know," she replied. "It was my sister's husband, the one I told you about. He says he can't find her. But I worry he's done something to her and is trying to act the grieving husband so no one will suspect him."

"I heard about a case on this true crime podcast I follow that's just like that," Penny said.

"That's what worries me."

Alejandra sighed and pulled up Rosaria's contact information on her phone. She clicked the little map icon and waited for the map application to open. Unbeknownst to Rosaria, the last time they had been together, Alejandra had gone into Rosaria's phone and shared her location, just in case.

The application showed a searching icon and then zoomed in on a pinned location. Alejandra recognized the location as the trailer right away. A text notification popped up announcing the phone had last pinged at that location on Saturday morning. The phone was currently offline.

"Are you okay?" Penny asked. "You suddenly went pale. Like your skin is my color right now."

Alejandra stared blankly ahead for a moment, then suddenly snapped into action. She grabbed her purse and phone and stood. "I need to go," she announced.

"Yeah, fine. Okay. I'll tell Zach you had a family emergency."

"Right. Good. Thanks." She strode purposefully towards the door.

"Call me if you need help," Penny called out.

# CHAPTER 27

## 1849

R ose found she was just able to fit into one of her old dresses and hurriedly put it on. They tackled the cabin first by dragging the dead horse thieves outside and laying them in a row at the front of the house.

"Looks like an ominous warning to anyone else passing by," Paul joked. "Don't mess with the cripple and his wife."

Rose tried to laugh, but she was staring at an army of ants attacking a pile of sugar on the ground. At least three bullets had punctured the barrel, and sugar poured out into little piles on the dirt floor. They were down half a barrel of sugar and now the barrel was no longer sealed.

She moved on to the flour barrel and found even worse news there. One of the boards had shattered, opening up the entire side. Flour mixed with the dirt floor in an unsalvageable mess. Only a few cups remained at the bottom of the barrel. She dragged the barrels to the back of the little cabin. She would have to deal with the food shortage later.

She took a straw broom and tried to sweep the spilled sugar and flour out through the door, but thick pools of blood just soaked up the dirt and powder. Paul stepped through the door.

"Okay?" he asked.

"Not really," she replied. "We have half a barrel of sugar and a few cups of flour left. Luckily, the salt seems to have survived intact."

"Well, that's something."

She grunted in response.

The front wall was dotted with bullet holes, a constellation of sunlight on the back wall.

"Where's the spade?" she asked. "I'm going to have to shovel this mess out of here."

"It's out by the corral." He paused. "Well, what used to be the corral. I'll get it."

They worked together in silence, both lost in their thoughts, cleaning and patching until Joseph woke from his nap. His cries filled the little cabin and Rose rushed to pick him up.

"Are you hungry?" she asked. She picked him up and immediately wrinkled her nose. "Oof. We need to change you first."

Rose changed him and carried him outside. She sat on the camp stool, which was somehow still sitting in front of the fire, and held him to her breast. Paul rounded the rock and joined them at the fire.

"What do you think about burying them under the tree back there?" he asked.

"The only one who deserves a proper Christian funeral is Sgt. Whitmer," she replied coldly.

"I don't disagree, but we don't want to attract scavengers either."

She sighed. "I guess not. Yes, that sounds fine. I can start digging when Joseph is finished." She looked up and instantly grew worried. Paul looked exhausted. His face was pale and clammy.

She immediately stood. "Sit down and rest. You have overexerted yourself."

"I'm fine," he argued weakly.

"You are definitely not fine. Sit."

Paul obeyed and slumped into the stool. He reached down and massaged his bad leg. "It does hurt a bit," he admitted.

"I'm so sorry," she said. "I should have realized you were doing too much. It's my fault." Visions of Paul lying in the back of the wagon, fighting for his life, flashed through her mind. She never wanted to go through that again.

"Don't worry. I just need a little rest."

When Joseph finished feeding, Rose handed him to Paul and got back to work. Her head hurt from where it banged against the rock, and she could feel Jed's hands wrapped around her wrists where bruises were starting to form, but she pushed the pain aside to accomplish what needed to be done.

She dragged the bodies one by one around the rock to the base of the tree. A dry wash ran in front of the tree, and the ground seemed softer there. She laid the bodies in a row along the banks of the wash, next to where she would dig their grave.

Her back ached from the work, and she dreaded the next step of shoveling a hole deep enough to bury the men. Her dress was drenched in sweat, and a slash of dirt painted her forehead where she had wiped the sweat out of her eyes. Paul stoked the fire and played with the baby while she worked.

She approached her two boys and smiled. Some color had returned to Paul's cheeks.

Suddenly, the ground shook and a deep rumble rolled across the valley just as they were cast into shadow. Paul and Rose looked at each other in surprise. She helped Paul to stand and they both looked off into the distance. Dark gray clouds filled the horizon.

"A storm's coming," Paul announced.

"I still need to get the two soldiers down from the rock," Rose said.

A gust of wind blew through the camp, carrying the clean scent of rain, as if announcing to the desert plants that life giving sustenance was on its way.

"The basin will fill with water, and the bodies will contaminate the pool," Rose said. "I need to get them down."

Paul looked back at the wall of rain quickly approaching. The wind was blowing harder now, and it carried away their words. "You don't have much time," he yelled.

He held Joseph close to his chest and pulled the blanket over his eyes. "Take the baby inside," Rose said. "I'll be right back."

Her skirts whipped around her legs, and her hair slapped wildly at her face. She hadn't put it up since dunking her head in the pool. She pulled her hair out of her eyes and held it back as she made her way to the crevice. The wind grew stronger, and she struggled to walk upright. When she reached the crevice, the wind calmed but made an otherworldly screeching noise as it rushed down through the narrow space.

Rose climbed as quickly as she could, dreading that she would have to look at the body of that evil man. When she reached the area surrounding the catch basin, the wind whistled overhead, but swirled gently in the protected space carved into the rock.

She stood over the body of Jed Jones and scowled. She spat on his face and tried to summon her hatred for the evil man. But she found the hatred wouldn't come. She felt disgust and contempt, but couldn't stoop to hatred, despite what he had done to her. As she worked through her thoughts and emotions, her shoulders slumped and she ultimately felt overwhelmed with pity for the man.

"Your soul is in hell now, suffering torment I could never imagine," she whispered. "I pray for your soul." With that, all emotion flushed from her body until she felt nothing. His body was just a clump of flesh, of clay—nothing more.

She heard Paul trying to yell to her over the wind, but couldn't make out his words. She scrambled up the rock face to the peak to get a better look and froze as soon as she reached the top.

The storm would hit any second. But it was like nothing she had ever seen. Lightning flashed inside angry roiling clouds the color of night. A solid wall of water stretched as far as she could see, like the entire ocean was about to crash down upon them in an instant. She looked down and saw Paul waving wildly, beckoning her to come down and find shelter with him in the cabin. Thunder cracked, rocking her back.

She signaled for Paul to go inside and slid down the rock face. She got to work, dragging Pvt. Jones by the feet to the crevice. A large step up blocked the entrance to the crevice, and she grunted as she pulled and pushed his limp body over the rock.

The rain hit, falling in driving sheets. She had seen rainstorms in Missouri, but nothing like this. The rain didn't fall in drops, but in shards that cut through her clothes and pounded against her skin as though it was desperate to beat the earth into submission. She could barely see a foot in front of her, but she noticed that the basin was close to overflowing and the water was steadily rising. By the time she reached Sgt. Whitmer, the water was lapping over her shoes.

She grabbed the sergeant's body by his hands and dragged him through the rising water. She had to stop frequently to wipe the water from her eyes. Her hair was plastered against her cheek. The pounding of the water against the rock drowned out any other sounds.

"Come on," she grunted as she tried to lift him over the step, but she couldn't even hear her own words. Exhausted, she leaned back against the wall and shivered. The water was at her shins and began to run across the top of the step and down into the crevice.

She felt a jolt of worry. "This is going to turn into a waterfall," she said. "And I will never make it down." She bent down and began again, struggling to pull the private through the narrow floor of the crevice. She soon realized that it was an impossible task. Without being able to carry him, he became wedged in the crevice and wouldn't budge.

"At least he's downhill from the catch basin," she told herself and returned to the top to try again with Sgt. Whitmer's body. As she worked, the water rose and began to flow rapidly down the crevice, pooling behind Pvt Jones. As she got close, she stepped into the rising water and her shoe caught on the edge of a rock. She slipped and she fell hard, landing on her shoulder.

Her momentum somehow dislodged Jones's body, and the sudden release of the pressure that had built up behind him sent a wave of water shooting down the crevice, taking Rose with it. She tumbled uncontrollably in the roiling wave, smashing against the rock walls until she landed with a thump at the bottom. A deluge of water continued to wash over her. Groaning, she opened her eyes and screamed. She was lying face to face on top of Pvt. Jones, his unseeing eyes staring blankly up at her.

She pushed away and rolled to the side, kicking and screaming until she managed to collapse a few feet away in the sand on her stomach, sobbing and unable to catch her breath. She could feel the ground underneath her being washed away by the storm, but she could no longer move. She commanded herself to get up and run to the cabin, but her limbs refused to obey. Every time she opened her mouth to catch her breath it filled with water, causing her to sputter and choke. She squeezed her eyes shut and focused on Joseph and Paul. She had to survive for them.

She managed to turn her head to the side and could just make out the corner of the cabin through the rain.

"Paul," she cried, but it was no use. If he hadn't heard her scream, he surely wouldn't hear her weak cries for help.

"Help me," she whispered. "Help."

# CHAPTER 28
## 2024

Rosaria felt the mountain close in around her and her entire world became the perimeter formed by the beam of her flashlight. She forced herself to stop thinking about what was lurking beyond her circle of light and climbed carefully down through the trees. She heard the menacing growl of the mountain lion playing on repeat in her mind, but refused to think about what could have happened had it decided to take refuge with her in the cavern.

The cold wind penetrated her coat and she shivered uncontrollably. Her brief moment of introspection at the top of the mountain had been cast aside by persistent pangs of thirst and hunger. Her mind wandered again.

*"Hey Francisco," Rosaria said shyly when he opened his front door.*

*"Hey. Come on in. We're up in the dining room," he responded and turned to lead the way up the stairs of the modest split level home.*

*She was the last to arrive and the others were talking excitedly about prom, their textbooks lying closed on the table. Rosaria sat down and nodded at the others in the group.*

"So are you going?" one of the kids asked.

"What? Oh, uhm, well no one has asked me yet," Rosaria replied. She glanced over at Francisco and felt her cheeks redden.

"What about you, Francisco?" one of the boys asked. "Have you asked Afton yet?"

Rosaria felt her heart quicken as she pleaded for him to say no.

"Not yet," he said with a grin. "But check this out." He got up and raced down the hall.

Rosaria slumped in her chair. Her plan had failed. He already had someone else in mind.

Francisco returned, carrying a white poster board. With a great flourish, he flipped it around and set it on the table. He had used candy bars taped to the board to form a message asking Afton to prom.

"What do you think?" he asked the group.

"Sweet," one of the boys responded.

The girl next to Rosaria nudged her with an elbow and leaned over to whisper in her ear. "Why does every boy think we want candy? Don't they know it's fattening?"

Rosaria faked a laugh and nodded her agreement. "I know, right?" She would have died to receive that invitation.

*Francisco took the poster board off the table and set it over on the kitchen counter. "I'm gonna deliver it to her house tonight after we're done," he announced. "So we better get busy."*

*The group formulated a plan and divided responsibilities for their project. They were required to build a diorama and write a report describing a specific part of the battle. Rosaria was assigned with building little houses out of popsicle sticks. She had agreed without argument, even though she would have rather been in charge of writing the report.*

*She snuck glances at Francisco throughout the evening. By the time they were done, she had almost convinced herself that he had smiled at her and would change his mind about Afton. She even day dreamed about Afton turning down his invitation and her coming to the rescue.*

*The evening passed in a blur, and she was surprised when Francisco announced he had to go or else Afton would be in bed and the raccoons would eat the candy bars. Rosaria gathered her things into her backpack and turned to leave, but felt someone tap her on the shoulder.*

*"Can I talk to you?" one of the boys in the group asked.*

*"Sure," she said as she tried to remember his name. Was it Jose? No, that wasn't it.*

*"Great." He looked at the others. "Outside?"*

*"Yeah, okay," she replied. Jorge! That was it.*

*When they got outside, Rosaria's mom was parked at the curb patiently waiting for her to be done. She turned to look at Jorge. "What is it?" she asked.*

*He looked down at his shoes and shuffled his feet. "Uhm, well..." he began.*

*Rosaria looked over at her mom and raised her finger. "One minute."*

*"Yes?"*

*"Well, I was wondering if you would go to prom with me. I heard you haven't been asked yet."*

*Rosaria stepped back in shock. She looked at the boy in front of her as if for the first time. He was kinda cute and seemed nice, and she knew Francisco wasn't going to ask her. Prom was only two weeks away and she didn't want to be the only junior without a date. All of these thoughts raced through her mind as he waited for her response.*

*Finally she blurted out her answer, "Sure, yeah."*

*He smiled and exhaled. "Great, Yeah, awesome. Okay, well, I'll see you in class." With that, he turned and ran across the yard, leaving Rosaria standing there wondering what had just happened.*

"And now Francisco and Afton have two kids and are involved in a heated divorce," Rosaria said bitterly. Alejandra had told her the news the last time they talked. "And look at me. I'm escaping over the mountain like some convict because my husband locked me in a bedroom for two days and threatened to beat me. What a life." She laughed, but it was devoid of humor.

She stepped over a protruding tree root and placed her hand against the trunk of the tree to steady herself.

"It could be worse, girl. You could be back home."

\*\*\*

Jorge tore out the dresser drawers, dumping their contents onto the bed while he searched for any kind of clue as to where his wife could have gone. He did the same to the closet, piling every item of clothing until he could barely reach the top.

He felt a familiar rage growing in his chest until he couldn't contain it any longer. He stormed into the nursery and began smashing and throwing the furniture against the thin trailer walls. The crib cracked apart, sending the spindles to the ground in a pile like a game of pick up sticks. He took one of the spindles and swung it like a bat at the changing table, screaming and swearing. He tore through the room until eventually he tired and came back to his senses, gasping for breath. He grunted when he saw the destruction in the room and dropped the spindle to the floor.

He left the room, closing the mess behind the door, and went into the bathroom to splash cold water on his face. It was there he found his first clue. Rosaria's toothbrush was gone along with the tube of toothpaste. That confirmed it. She had left him.

"You don't get to just leave me like she did," he hissed. "You're mine."

The sudden familiar feeling of abandonment pierced his heart and he felt panic rising in his chest. He tried to push away the painful memory of a different reflection from long ago, but his attempt was futile.

*An all too familiar little boy stared back at him. His hair was unkempt and a smudge of something dark was smeared across his cheek where he had wiped away a tear. A severe looking woman appeared behind the little boy, her gray hair pulled into a tight bun. "Come on, let's go," she said in a no nonsense tone. "Grab your toothbrush."*

*The little boy started to cry. "I want my mommy."*

*She scowled and grabbed him by the arm. "Your mother isn't coming back," she said coldly. "She's in jail where women like her belong."*

*"No. She needs to read us a story."*

*His younger sister appeared behind the woman, clinging tightly to her skirt. "What's wrong?" she asked in a scared little voice.*

*"You're going to a new family," the woman said. She pulled him roughly away from the sink. "Let's go. They're waiting to meet you."*

*"But she won't know where we are. How will she know where to come get us?" the boy asked.*

*"She's not coming back," the woman replied coldly. "Just forget about her."*

*He tried to pull away but her fingers clamped around his arm until he felt the painful bite of her nails.*

*His younger sister wailed.*

*"Now look at what you've done," the woman said. "If you don't*

*behave, your new family won't want you either."*

*The little boy hung his head in defeat and let the woman lead him away.*

The water was still running, and Jorge put his palms under the flow and bent over. He splashed his face and rubbed away the vision. He had sworn that day that no one would ever abandon him again.

He went outside and circled the trailer, trying to think. What would Rosaria do? Where would she go? She couldn't drive. Her sister didn't save her. She didn't have enough money for a taxi or a ride share. She could have made it into town and taken a bus.

He found himself standing in the backyard at the property line, staring across the valley at the mountains beyond.

"Who in town would have helped her?" he asked. "Melanie? No, or else she should be an actress. She seemed surprised."

He looked down at the ground, and it took a moment for him to register what he was seeing. As plain as day, a set of footprints impressed in the dirt led off into the desert.

"No way," he said, looking from the footprints to the mountains and back. "She wouldn't have the balls."

He stepped over the fence and followed the tracks into the desert. Sure enough, they continued on as far as he could see.

"Gotcha!" he exclaimed.

He raced back to the trailer and grabbed the keys to his dirt bike from a nail on the wall. He rolled the bike out of the shed and checked the gas tank—full. He climbed onto the bike and, for a split second, thought he should gather some supplies before he left.

"Nah," he said and pulled out the clutch. "I'll catch up to her in no time." He stomped down on the kickstarter and the bike roared to life.

# CHAPTER 29

# 1849

R ose blinked and spat sand from her mouth. Her head was pounding.

"Rose, Rose, you're awake." Paul gushed. "I was so worried."

Rose pushed herself up and squinted against the bright sunlight. A blurry image of her husband slowly came into focus.

"Joseph?" she asked.

"He's fine," Paul assured her. He helped her get up on her knees.

"What happened?" she asked. She looked around and started in surprise. The desert seemed to have come alive. Little specks of green poked through the dirt all around her, and flowers bloomed brightly in the sunlight where none had been before.

"The rain, I guess," Paul explained.

Rose felt the grit of sand scratching against her teeth as she talked; she tried to spit it out.

The back of her dress was dry where it was exposed to the sun, but the front was still wet where she had lain on her stomach.

"Do you remember anything?" Paul asked gently, pointing behind her.

She glanced back and saw the bodies of Pvt. Jones and Sgt. Whitmer tangled together in a heap. She tried to focus but still felt woozy.

"Oh, right, I forgot." Paul picked up a tin cup beside him and placed it in her hands. Shakily, she took a sip, swished it about, and spat it out. She then took a long drink of the cool water.

"Thanks," she sighed. "That's better." She pushed herself up and managed to stand. Paul used his crutch to get to his feet.

She looked at the crevice and then back at the bodies. "I remember the rain. It was coming down so hard that it filled the entire basin like a bowl of soup in no time. I was trying to drag their bodies down the crevice, when Pvt. Jones got jammed against the rock. Then…"

"It's okay. Take your time."

"Then I went back for Sgt. Whitmer. He was too heavy to lift, so I was dragging him too and I slipped and then it was like I went tumbling down a roaring river and…" She shivered as a vision of Pvt. Jones' blank stare flooded her memory. "I felt like I was drowning and I couldn't get myself to move, and then, well, then you woke me up."

Paul sighed with frustration. "This damn leg. If I could have helped you, none of this would have happened."

"Paul, stop. We are just grateful that you're alive." She changed the subject. "How did the house fare in the storm?"

"Hah! Well, the roof held out for a little bit, but eventually it turned to mud and started washing away. The wind blew the rain through the gaps and under the wall so the entire place is a muddy mess. I managed to get the blankets onto the table so they're wet, but not too muddy."

"Was little Joseph scared?"

"He slept through the whole thing, actually."

They both laughed. Oh, to be a baby.

"We need to get Pvt. Jones here back with the others and start digging," Rose said.

"You're exhausted and almost drowned. They can wait."

"Not with those coyotes out there, they can't. Come on, you can help me."

As they approached the wash behind the tree with Pvt. Jones, Rose gasped. The bank had eroded away, and the horse thieves were nowhere to be found. The high water mark was clearly visible where the flash flood had deposited branches and rocks. It was well above where she had placed the other men.

"Oh no!" she exclaimed.

Paul grunted. "That solves that problem," he said.

"Paul, that's awful."

"Sorry. I don't feel bad for them. I'll go get the spade." He turned and hobbled away.

Rose noticed a mark carved into the base of the standing rock under the gnarled branches of the piñon pine. She stepped closer and knelt down to run her fingers over the inscription. The carving was shallow, eroded with time, but still barely visible in the filtered light under the tree.

"It's a man," Rose said. "And he's carrying something." The carving must have been uncovered by the rainstorm as sand and dirt washed away from the base of the pillar. Rose pushed away the top layer of sand, eager to clear the area for greater visibility. She found writing in an unknown language carved into the surface under the man.

Her nails scratched against something solid in the earth just as Paul returned with the spade.

"What are you doing?" he asked.

"Come, look at this," she said excitedly.

Paul approached and carefully knelt next to her. "What is it?"

"I don't know, a carving of some kind. And look, here, at the writing. I don't recognize it. Do you?"

"It's not English, that's for sure, but I can't say what it is. Maybe it's the language of one of the local tribes."

"Give me the spade," she ordered.

"He handed it to her and watched as she carefully dug and scraped to uncover whatever was buried at the base of the carvings. As she worked, a flat stone emerged out of the sand, clearly smoothed and shaped by man based on the visible tool marks. It sat at a gradual slope from the sheer vertical wall of the rock, as if the rock formation widened at the base, but had been buried by sand over time. After a few minutes of vigorous work clearing around the edges of the rectangular object, she brushed away any last grains of sand with her hand and sat back.

In the center of the stone, the artist had carved a column of pictographs featuring the sun at the top, then the moon, and finally a star. Rose ran a finger lightly over the carving.

What do you think it means?" she asked.

# CHAPTER 30
## 2024

J orge sped through the desert as fast as he could while still following Rosaria's tracks. He could tell that she was headed for the mountains, so he frequently sped forward before circling around to ensure he was still on her trail.

The wind whipped through his hair and stung his eyes, but anger deadened any discomfort.

When he reached the first foothill, he saw that she had hiked straight up the hill, so without thinking, he gunned the engine and followed suit.

The steep hill proved too much for his bike, and it stalled before he reached the halfway point. He knew that he wasn't an expert rider, but he still felt embarrassed enough to look around and ensure no one saw his failed attempt to climb. He struggled to turn the bike on the steep hill. As he tried to maneuver the machine around, the tires began slipping in the sand, threatening to send the bike careening down the hill.

Jorge panicked and jumped free, letting the bike fall to its side and slide. He landed with his hand in the middle of a cholla cactus and filled the air with obscenities directed at Rosaria. He sat in the dirt and picked at the little thorns stuck in his palm with his fingernails.

The tedious work fed his anger until he finally took out his pocketknife and scraped the edge roughly against his palm over and over until the last thorn finally broke free. He clenched his fingers into a fist and then opened them for a final inspection.

"I think I got them all," he said.

He slid down to where his bike was laying sideways in the dirt and wrestled to pull it to a standing position. He wheeled it across the face of the hill until he reached the dirt road that led up to the cell phone tower. He climbed on and rode the rest of the way on the gradual switchbacks.

He leaned his bike against the brick building and scanned the area. Rosaria's footprints climbed up over the top of the hill but disappeared on the gravel surrounding the building. What little knowledge he had about tracking came from watching hunting videos online, but he examined the area like he knew exactly what he was looking for.

He got lucky. On the concrete pad next to the building, he found a dried patch of white spittle. He ran a finger over the substance and held it to his nose.

"Toothpaste." Next to the stain, a little piece of wrapper clung to the mortar between the blocks. He pulled it free and examined it. He wasn't sure what it was but just knew it came from his wife.

"She must have spent the night here," he concluded.

Night was falling, but Jorge felt he was close to catching his prey.

"No point stopping now," he declared, mounting the bike.

*** 

Rosaria made good time by the light of the flashlight until the light flickered and dimmed. She slapped the flashlight against her palm like she had seen people do in the movies, but it did nothing. She hurried to find a spot at the base of a pine tree where the ground was relatively flat.

By the dimming light of the torch, she brushed away pebbles and pinecones to make herself a smooth bed of pine needles. She zipped up her coat and pulled the blanket up to her chin, but doing so exposed her feet. She readjusted the blanket and curled into the fetal position, using her backpack as a pillow.

She desperately wanted to remove her shoes and let her feet breath, but was afraid of what she would find. The blisters on her heels had popped earlier in the day giving some relief, but not much. The open sores still chafed painfully with every step. Her feet felt swollen and tight in her boots, and she feared she wouldn't be able to get them back on if she took them off.

And more importantly, she wanted to be able to move quickly should danger arise. Ultimately, she decided to put up with the discomfort and leave them on.

She closed her eyes and sighed.

"You made it over the mountain," she whispered to herself. "You're more than halfway there."

She imagined what Jorge must have done when he found her gone and shuddered. "You can never go back. He'll kill you."

As she faded off to sleep, her mind wandered back.

*After asking her to prom, Jorge seemed to avoid talking to her at school. He rushed out of class everyday and turned around in the hallway when she approached.*

*"Do you think he was serious?" Rosaria asked Lupe the next week. They were standing next to their lockers. Jorge had just turned the corner, looked up, and immediately disappeared back around the corner. "He hasn't said a word to me since he asked me. I don't even know if we're going to dinner or if our colors match or anything."*

*"He's a little weird," Lupe observed. "But he's kinda cute."*

*"I just need to corner him and talk to him," Rosaria decided, closing her locker door.*

*"He has a sister," Lupe said. "You could ask her what's going on."*

*"That's not a bad idea. Who's his sister?"*

*"Her name's Soledad. She's in my art class, next period actually.*

*Do you want me to talk to her?"*

*Rosaria thought about it for a second. She had English next and her teacher loved her. He wouldn't mind if she was a few minutes late just this once. "No, I'll go with you. Just point her out to me."*

*Soledad was already seated at her table, arranging colored pencils in a neat row above her project when they arrived. Lupe tapped her on the shoulder and pointed to Rosaria who stood in the doorway. Soledad sighed and agreed to talk, following Lupe to the door.*

*"Thanks, Lupe," Rosaria said. When Lupe didn't move, Rosaria gave her a look and a little push. Lupe got the message and went into class.*

*"Hey, sorry. I'm Rosaria."*

*"I know. Jorge told me he asked you to prom."*

*"Yeah, so..."*

*"You're not going to back out, are you?" Soledad interrupted, a worried look on her face.*

*Rosaria frowned. "No, why?"*

*"Okay, phew, just checking."*

*"Okay, well, no I'm not backing out, but I'm worried Jorge is. He hasn't said one word to me since he asked me and I need to know his plans so I can get my dress and tell my parents what we're doing. Are we going with a group? Are we going to dinner? Is there*

*a day-date planned? Like, what's going on?"*

*Soledad puffed her cheeks and exhaled. She shook her head, like she was used to having to fix Jorge's dating life.* "No, sorry. He's *just super shy and a little freaked out that he actually asked you. I told him that he needs to talk to you, and he said he would. But I'm not surprised that he hasn't."*

*The bell rang and a few stragglers rushed past them into class.*

"Look, I doubt he will want to go with a group. He does better *without crowds. But I will get him to talk to you. I promise."*

"Ok, thanks. Like, I don't wanna be rude, but my parents won't *let me go if I can't tell them what we're doing."*

"I get it. He just gets worried that people are going to bail on him, *so he got a little freaked out. Long story, but..."*

"Miss Castro, the bell rang," *the art teacher said.*

"Yeah. Coming," *she replied.*

"I need to talk to him, like, soon."

"Don't worry. I'll tell him. He will."

Rosaria yawned. "Red flag number three hundred and forty-two," she mumbled. "Fear of rejection." She shivered and pulled herself into a tighter ball.

# CHAPTER 31

# 1849

E verything else forgotten, Rose and Paul excitedly studied their new find.

"I think it's a lid or door of some kind," Paul suggested. He grabbed the spade and began digging around the edge of the flat stone. "It almost looks like the cellar door back home, except it's made of stone."

"Do you remember the time we had to hide in the cellar when the tornado was spotted across Mr. Peterson's field?"

"I sure do. I'm glad it didn't do any more damage than it did."

Rose turned her attention back to the stone. "Can you see a seam between the top and the sides?" Rose asked. She bent over to get a better look. "Here, try to get the spade into this little crack here." She pointed to a thin line, only visible at the right angle. "I think this might be a seam."

Paul tried, but the spade's blade was too thick, and there seemed to be something sealing the lid to the rest of the box.

"It won't budge. We need a knife or something to cut through the lip here," Paul said.

"There was a bowie knife on the ground in the cabin I found when I was cleaning up," Rose suggested.

"That was Sgt. Whitmer's," Paul explained. "He came into the cabin with it, and the other guy knocked him out cold before I..." He paused, mid sentence, remembering that horrible moment.

Rose took his hand in hers and waited for him to finish.

"Before I killed a man," he finally said.

"Before you saved his life, and ultimately my life." She took his other hand and looked him in the eye. "You did what you had to do for your family," Rose said.

Paul bowed his head with mixed emotion. "I know that; I do. But I still killed a man, and that is, I don't know. I never expected it to be like this." He shook his head and sniffed. "Sorry. My weakness must disgust you."

"Stop," she said firmly. "You did the right thing."

He smiled weakly.

She leaned him and gave him a quick kiss. "I'll go get the knife." She stood and stretched her back from being hunched over so long. "Joseph is probably wondering where we are by now, too. And, we still need to give Sgt. Whitmer a proper Christian burial before it gets dark."

"What about Pvt. Jones here?"

"He's last in line."

# CHAPTER 32

## 2024

The terrain quickly grew too rough to ride his bike. Too stubborn to admit he hadn't thought this through, Jorge abandoned the bike next to a large boulder and continued on foot.

It wasn't long before he heard voices coming towards him, and two men walked around a bend.

They stopped short when they saw Jorge, surprised someone else would be up on the mountain that late in the day. The three men assessed each other before Jorge spoke.

"Hey, Doug, what are you doing up here? The boss said you went hunting."

Doug looked at Scott, who, after a moment's hesitation, nodded.

"We did go hunting," Scott replied, grinning. He turned around to show off the mountain lion pelt tied to his pack.

"You got a mountain lion? Are those in season?" Jorge asked dumbly.

Scott frowned. "It tried to attack us," he explained. "Self-defense." He didn't mention the fact they had shot at and wounded the cat first.

"You look a little pale, Doug. You all right?"

"Yeah, I'm fine. Our truck's just around the corner there."

Jorge frowned. "I didn't see any truck that way."

"Are you kidding me?" Doug asked, speaking more to Scott than to Jorge. "You promised we were on the right trail this time, you idiot. We've been wandering around all day looking for the stupid truck."

"I swear," Scott protested. "It's right around the corner. You must have just missed it, Jorge."

Jorge grunted. "Whatever."

Doug groaned and grabbed his shoulder. "Cat scratched me," he explained. "I'm afraid it's getting infected because this moron left the first aid kit in the truck that he can't seem to find."

Jorge chuckled. That was the first funny thing he'd heard all day—all weekend in fact.

"It's not really funny," Doug protested.

Scott looked Jorge up and down. "What are you doing up here, anyway?" he asked. "Without any gear or nothin'."

Jorge debated what to say, but decided that if the two men had been wandering all over the mountain side all day, they may have seen something.

"I'm looking for my wife, Rosaria. She, uh, she went on a hike this morning and hasn't come back yet. You know, I'm worried about her."

"She the one who works at the dollar store?" Doug asked.

"You know that," Scott said, smacking him on the shoulder.

Doug cried out in pain.

"Oh, sorry man."

"So?" Jorge asked. "Have you seen her?"

The two hunters looked at each other and both shrugged.

"Nah, man," Scott replied. "We haven't seen another human all day until you showed up."

"Okay, thanks. Hey, you got an extra flashlight on you I can use? I want to keep searching. Don't want her stuck up here overnight you know."

"Sure," Scott said. "Here, it's in the side pocket."

Jorge approached the men and unzipped the side pocket of Scott's pack. He found a thin flashlight and zipped the pocket closed.

"Thanks." Jorge stepped back. An idea began forming in his mind, and he debated for a second while the men stared at him quizzically. He decided to go for it. "I'm getting worried, with it getting dark and all. Do you think when you guys get home that you could call my godfather, Officer Gonzalez, and have him organize a search party? You know, just in case we're not home by tomorrow morning?"

Scott hemmed and hawed, not excited about talking to the cops, especially with a poached mountain lion in his possession.

"You don't have to file a report or anything. Just tell him you ran into me and I asked him to check the house in the morning to see if we're back."

"Yeah, we can do that, no problem," Doug finally said. "As long as we make it off this stupid mountain ourselves."

"Give it a rest, man. The truck is right down there, I swear."

Jorge watched as the two men disappeared down the trail. The more he thought about it, the more he liked the plan. He would find Rosaria first, show her exactly what happens to someone who abandons him, and then join the search party as the frantically worried husband. It would be perfect.

*** 

Alejandra pulled into the driveway and parked next to Jorge's truck. Her stomach felt tied in knots in apprehension at having to confront Jorge in person. She took a deep breath and climbed out of her car.

"I'm done," she said as she marched to the door. "I've sat back and watched him hurt my sister for long enough." She pounded on the door with her fist. "Jorge, let me in."

Dried leaves tumbled across the yard as a light breeze swirled around her. She knocked again, remembering with guilt a previous conversation with her sister.

> "He treats you like garbage. He's a jerk," Alejandra said. They were walking down the aisle of a baby discount store looking for a cheap stroller.

> Rosara ignored her and ran her hand over one of the floor models. "This one looks nice." She lifted the price tag and frowned.

*Alejandra stepped in and checked the price. "That's fine. I told you that I was going to buy the stroller for you. It's my baby gift."*

*"I know, but that's too much."*

*"You don't get to decide. It's a gift."*

*Rosaria placed her hand on Alejandra's arm and smiled. "Thank you."*

*"You didn't answer me," Alejandra prodded.*

*"What was the question again?"*

*Alejandra sighed in exasperation. "Do you really want him raising your baby? What if he treats the baby like he treats you?"*

*"He's just stressed. Money's tight. I'm sure he will change when he sees the baby."*

*Alejandra laughed dryly. "I've heard that before. He'll change when we get married. He'll change when we find a place of our own. He'll change when he gets a job. Has he ever changed? No!"*

*"That's not fair. He loves me. He does. It's just, he doesn't know how. I mean, he had a hard childhood."*

*"Yes, I know. So have a lot of other people. But they don't punch their wives."*

*"That was an accident," Rosaria protested.*

*"No it wasn't, and you know it."*

*Rosaria began to cry, and Alejandra pulled her into a hug. Another shopper walked by, staring. Alejandra smiled and mouthed "Hormones." The woman nodded and smiled sympathetically.*

*When she had gone, Alejandra pulled back, her hands on Rosaria's shoulders. "I'm sorry sis, we're supposed to be having fun shopping. I just, well, I worry about you and the baby."*

*"I know. And I know it's not right, okay. I do. But I don't have anywhere to go where he won't get to me. If I'm there, I can maybe manage him. If I leave, I don't know what he'll do."*

*"He needs to be in prison."*

*"If I complain to the police, he'll kill me. And anyway, his godfather is an officer. They'll never believe me over him."*

*"You can come to our house any time."*

*"That will put you and your kids in danger."*

*"I don't care."*

*"Well, I do. Just trust me, okay? Let me do it my way."*

*Alejandra sighed and slid her hands down until she held Rosaria's. She squeezed. "Just do it before it's too late, yeah?"*

*Rosaria nodded silently, then turned back to the stroller. "This one is great," she said. "Should we ask if they have one in a box?"*

*Alejandra surreptitiously wiped her eyes. "Yeah, I'll go find some-
one."*

No one came to the door, so Alejandra tried the knob—unlocked. She
stepped inside. "Jorge? Are you here? Rosaria?"

The trailer was quiet other than the hum of the furnace kicking on in the cool
afternoon.

# CHAPTER 33
# 1849

They wrapped Sgt. Whitmer's body in a blanket and rolled it into the shallow grave. Paul said a few words before Rose began refilling the hole. They had chosen a spot under the shadow of the rock where the horses used to be stabled.

"I'll grab some driftwood from the wash out back and we can fashion a cross for his grave," Rose said. She wiped the sweat from her brow. She felt dirty and grimy. The pale skin of her neck had turned an angry red from bending over to dig with her hair pulled up into a bun. She felt sand in her every joint and crevice. Memories of the big wash basin her mother used to bring out on Saturday nights flooded her mind, and she could almost feel the hot water and rough lye soap against her skin.

"When we get to town, I am going to pay for the hottest bath I can stand, and I'm going to soak in that water until my fingers turn to prunes."

"What did you say?" Paul asked.

"Nothing darling. I was just daydreaming about taking a nice hot bath."

"That sounds wonderful," Paul replied. He lifted one arm and sniffed, recoiling immediately. "I may need two."

"These are the best two branches I could find. Do you want to carve his name and the date on this one and I'll find some rope and a nail to lash them together in a cross?"

"Sure." Paul hobbled over to the camp stool and sat down.

Rose handed him Sgt. Whitmer's bowie knife and he began to carve as Rose started to prepare some food for dinner.

"We don't have much food left, what with the shot up barrels" she said as she stirred the pot over the fire.

"Yet another reason for us to get out of here," Paul said. "We can't carry anything on foot anyway."

"Paul, what are we going to do once we get to Santa Fe? We have no supplies, no food, and winter is coming fast."

"We still have a little money hidden in the cabin. We'll figure something out. I promise."

Rose continued to stir the stew. Both lost in their thoughts, they worked in silence side by side, the only sounds being the crackle of the fire, the gurgling stew, and the scrape of the knife against the wood.

"Paul..."

"Rose..."

They both spoke at once, stopped and tried again.

"You go," Rose said, deferring to her husband.

"If this foot doesn't get better soon, I'll have to figure out something I can do for work."

"You always said that you wanted to take the bar exam," Rose replied. "You've read all of the books. You know the law. You can start a law practice."

Paul thought about it. "Hmmm," he said. "I could do that. But what if there's already a lawyer in town?"

"Well, you could read for him, take the bar, and become a partner. You don't need to be able to run a mile as a lawyer."

"But I'd still need to be able to put in our crops and do the chores around the house," he protested.

"I can help with those. We are in this together."

"But, you didn't marry a cripple. It's not fair to you if..."

"Paul, no more talk like that. I married you, for better or worse. We will do this—together. Now finish up. Supper's ready."

After supper, Rose took the spade and went back to the wash near the piñon to dig a shallow grave for Pvt. Jones. She took a break when she finished digging the hole and looked out across the valley to the mountains beyond, leaning on the handle of the shovel. They would have to travel through those mountains on foot. To her surprise, she realized that the mountain peaks were dusted white with snow from the recent storm. Winter was just around the corner.

"We're out of time," she said as she rolled Pvt. Jones unceremoniously into the shallow grave. She considered saying a few words over his grave, but decided against it. With her thoughts focused on her upcoming travel preparations, she returned to the cabin to get ready for bed.

# CHAPTER 34
## 2024

Rosaria gradually awoke to the sound of a bird trilling in the branches above her. She looked up and saw a flash of red hop from one branch to another. Pink and orange painted the sky in broad brush strokes as dawn approached.

Her stomach rumbled and she pulled the pack from beneath her head to grab some food until she remembered that she was out. Her heart sank at the prospect of another day hiking without food or water. Every ounce of her screamed to just lie back down and sleep.

"No," she blurted out. "You didn't come this far to only quit now. You can't give Jorge the satisfaction. Get your butt up and get going."

The bird trilled again in support, or maybe it just wanted the human intruder to leave. Either way, its message was clear: time to move on.

She stretched her aching joints and licked her chapped lips. Her skin prickled, and every nerve seemed to crackle with sensitivity. Her clothes felt like sandpaper against her skin, stiff and grimy.

In a sudden frenzy, she pulled her shirt over her head and reached into her pack for her only other clean shirt, the one she had been saving to wear after she had cleaned herself up a bit to look presentable to passing motorists on the highway. But she didn't care anymore. She couldn't wear her dirty blouse for another second. She unclasped her bra and stuffed it into the pack with the dirty blouse and quickly pulled on the clean garment.

She felt goosebumps pop overall over her back as the cold fabric touched her skin. She shivered and sighed. The clean shirt felt glorious. She looked down at her pants, the urge to change her pants and underwear just as strong. But then she remembered her feet and decision to keep her shoes on.

She scratched her pants over her thighs to try and ease the itchy discomfort. A new blouse would have to suffice. She pulled the backpack on, kicked the little nest of needles she had used as a bed, and started down the mountain.

She hiked for hours as the sun rose to its zenith in the sky. Her knees shook with every step down the steep slope on what passed for a trail. "This trail is only fit for goats," she mumbled. Her thighs burned, her head throbbed, and her tongue felt swollen with thirst.

She began searching her memory for survival tips she may have gleaned from television shows and movies but couldn't remember any details that matched her situation. She scanned the hillside below looking for any signs of water, but nothing jumped out at her. Pushing herself onward, she forced her mind to wander to stop the persistent demands for water.

*Jorge picked her up for prom in his uncle's Mustang. He knocked quietly on the door and stared at the floor as Rosaria's mom tried to keep him entertained while they waited for Rosaria to finish getting ready.*

*Finally, Rosaria appeared at the top of the stairs. She paused for a moment, modeling the satin dress she had found in the thrift shop next to the county employment center. Her aunt, a talented seamstress, had worked on it every night that week. Rosaria had nervously waited to see the result, praying the dress wouldn't look like a thrift store find.*

*Her aunt had worked a miracle, adding just the right touches to make the dress fit perfectly on Rosaria's skinny frame. She and Alejandra spent all afternoon doing her nails and hair. She felt beautiful and confident as she presented herself at the top of the stairs.*

*Her mom gasped and clapped as Rosaria descended, and she beamed with happiness. She looked at Jorge to gauge his reaction, but couldn't tell what he was thinking. When she got down to the landing, she spun in a circle and waited for a compliment that never came.*

*Her mom noticed the uncomfortable silence and stepped in. "You look beautiful dear," she said. "Doesn't she, Jorge?"*

*"Yes ma'am," he replied. He looked at Rosaria again and smiled shyly.*

*Relief washed through her.*

*"You look nice, too," Rosaria said. She reached out and straightened his tie. He flinched but then caught himself and allowed her to finish.*

*"Uh, thanks. We better go."*

*"Not before I take a few pictures," her mom said.*

*Rosaria rolled her eyes, but was secretly pleased. She wanted to always remember how pretty she felt at that moment.*

*When they got in the car, Rosaria turned to Jorge. "Are we meeting the others at the restaurant?" she asked.*

*Jorge frowned.*

*"We are going with your friends, aren't we?"*

*He shook his head. "I just want to be with you," he said. "We don't need anyone else." He glanced at the clock on the dashboard. "We're going to be late for the restaurant. We were supposed to leave right at five."*

*"Oh, sorry," Rosaria said. I should have listened to Alejandra and not worried about my hair, she thought.*

*"It's fine," he said flatly as he looked over his shoulder and backed out of the driveway.*

*They ate alone at the restaurant, at first sitting in awkward silence until Rosaria began asking Jorge questions about himself. He explained that he and his sister weren't from the area, but had been placed in a foster home there. He answered every question with one word until she finally hit a subject that piqued his interest. When she asked about the Mustang, his eyes lit up and he began talking about model years, paint colors, and engine sizes—all things Rosaria knew nothing about. Happy that she had finally cracked through his hard exterior, she was content to eat and listen to him ramble on about cars.*

*It wasn't until months later that she realized that he had never once asked her a question about herself. In fact, he didn't show any interest in what she liked or how she felt.*

"Red flags six hundred seventy-two and three," she mumbled as she stopped for a rest on a boulder. "I was so naive."

She had made good time and could finally see the valley floor below. She looked out across the valley and noticed a speck in the distance moving across the valley floor. The unnaturally straight line of a road cut the valley in half.

Her heart leapt. "The highway!" she exclaimed. "You're almost there." She stared at a rock formation standing alone in the center of the valley. "That's your reference point. Keep that straight ahead and you'll make it to the road."

The vehicle finished its journey across the valley and climbed out of sight through the pass on the southern end. She stood there for a moment, waiting to see if any other cars would appear traveling north in the direction of Colorado. The road remained empty.

***

Alejandra awoke with a start at the sound of a car door slamming out in the yard. She wiped her eyes and pulled herself up from the sagging couch. Someone knocked on the door. *Not Jorge or Rosaria, then*, she thought.

She had waited up for either Jorge or Rosaria to return home, but finally fell asleep on the couch in the early hours of the morning.

The person knocked again.

"Just a second," she replied. She pulled her hair back into a ponytail and used a rubber band from around her wrist to secure it. She pulled open the door to find a police officer standing on the step, his fist raised to knock again.

The officer frowned. "Who are you?" he demanded. He pushed his way inside and looked around the front room.

"I'm Alejandra, Rosaria's sister." A jolt of fear shot through her and she felt the adrenaline snapping her awake. "Why? What happened? Is something wrong?"

The officer ignored her questions. "Are Rosaria and Jorge here?" he asked.

"No, officer. I was actually going to call you guys if they weren't back by morning. Wait, why are you here again?"

The officer strode down the hall, opening each door and glancing inside as he passed. It didn't take long to search the small trailer and he returned a minute later. "What happened back there?" he asked, thumbing a finger down the hall.

"What do you mean?"

"Someone destroyed the baby's room, and the bedroom's a mess."

"It is? I mean, I don't know. I never went back there. I've been waiting for Jorge to come home all night."

The officer eyes her suspiciously, waiting for her to continue.

"Jorge called me yesterday saying Rosaria didn't go to work and wasn't at home, so I got worried and drove out here. I got here last night and no one was home."

"He didn't say that she went hiking?"

"Hiking? What? No. Rosaria doesn't hike."

"Hmmm," the officer responded.

Alejandra found her glasses on the counter and put them on. She read the name badge on the officer's chest. Gonzalez. *Is that the name of Jorge's godfather?*

Officer Gonzalez went to the fridge and took out a can of soda. He pulled back the tab and took a long drink. Alejandra frowned.

"He said he didn't know where Rosaria was. He called me because Soledad told him that she found a note from Rosaria saying she was going to my house. But that's not true. I was in Amarillo all weekend with my husband."

"Jorge, Jorge," Officer Gonzalez mumbled before taking another drink.

"You still haven't told me why the police are here. Did something happen?"

Officer Gonzalez took a moment to reappraise her before answering. "I need to verify who you are before I answer your questions. Do you have any ID?"

Alejandra rushed to her wallet lying on the floor at the foot of the couch and dug out her driver's license. She handed it to Officer Gonzalez and he stepped outside while talking to the radio mic clipped to his left epaulet. Alejandra paced back and forth while she waited for him to return.

"Okay, everything checks out," he announced, handing her back the license.

"And?"

"Oh, yeah. Sorry, I just realized Jorge's truck is parked out front and was wondering how it got here. His license is suspended."

"From the DUI? Yeah, he told me about that."

"Right. Well, anyway. We had two citizens come in this morning to report that they ran into Jorge up in the mountains last night and he asked them to ask me to check on them this morning."

"What was he doing in the mountains?"

"Jorge told the guys that his wife went on a hike and hadn't come home, so he was out looking for her. But he had to borrow a flashlight and didn't have any supplies so he said if they weren't home by this morning, we should send out a search and rescue party."

"Was he drunk again?"

"That I don't know. But, it looks like they aren't back."

Alejandra hesitated for a moment. "Maybe Jorge knows exactly what happened to Rosaria and was just trying to create an alibi or something?"

"What do you mean by that?"

"He's not exactly a loving husband," Alejandra said, watching to judge Officer Gonzalez's reaction.

He frowned. "I'm not sure I like what you're implying about my godson, Miss."

"We just need to find them," Alejandra said.

They stood staring at each other.

"Well, let's go!" Alejandra finally said. "Let's get the search team organized."

"You don't think that Jorge would really...?" He couldn't finish the question.

"We better pray that he wouldn't. Now, get on that radio of yours."

# CHAPTER 35
## 1849

They slept huddled close under blankets still damp from the monsoon. Dark visions flashed through Rose's mind everytime she closed her eyes—Pvt. Jones' dark eyes inches from her face, his rotting teeth and foul breath, his grimy hands pawing all over her body, and Sgt. Whitmer's eyes rolling back in his head before he slumped to the ground. She forced herself to think of something good and beautiful, like her mother's garden, the apple blossoms in the spring, or little Joseph. But everytime she filled her thoughts with beauty, the darkness crept in and infected the scene with blackness.

She stared at the canvas ceiling. With most of the mud washed away, the moon's glow filtered through the cloth. Joseph breathed loudly through his nose, gurgling every so often. Rose wondered what dreams filled his head. Would he remember the things he saw today?

She worried that her son would bear the scars of the day, and was determined to hide her own pain from him. He needed her to be his mother and keep him safe, not to fall apart.

Her thoughts drifted to their escape. They had waited long enough. If another wagon train was going to pass through, it would have done so already. They were usually only a few weeks behind, and more than a month had passed. Their deadline was fast approaching.

Without horses, they had no other choice but to walk. Normally, that wouldn't be a problem. She had walked everywhere her entire life. She had walked for miles and miles alongside the wagons on the trail, chatting with the other wives and searching for beneficial plants and herbs. But they had a wagon to carry their things, especially water. Now, they could only carry so much and pray that it was enough to get them to the next water hole. And with Paul's foot, he wouldn't be able to carry as much as they needed him to.

She calculated in her mind what she would bring. She could tie little Joseph in the sling and carry a pack on her back with water, food, and some tools. Paul could use a feed bag tied over his shoulder for some additional supplies, but despite his protests, he was still too weak to carry much. He would never complain to her, but she knew that he still tired quickly. The journey could kill him.

*Maybe we could just talk with the Apache and ask for more time*, she thought briefly before dismissing the idea. *No, they were very clear. We must go.*

Even though the journey would be dangerous, their window to leave was quickly slipping away. Winter in the high desert could be rough, and with their dwindling supplies, they wouldn't last until spring. They had no choice.

Rose glanced over at Paul in the moonlight. His face was relaxed and free from pain or discomfort. She prayed that she would see that face in the daylight once again some day soon.

"Please God," she whispered. "We need your help."

# CHAPTER 36
## 2024

By the time Jorge admitted to himself his mistake in not turning back for supplies, it was too late. Tired, hungry, and thirsty, he found himself fueled onward by his temper. He kept hiking, focusing his discomfort on his wife. It was all her fault, after all.

If she had just put away the crib when he told her to, he wouldn't have had to lock her in the room.

If she had stayed home and gone to work like a good girl, they would both be home in bed. She could have welcomed him home from jail properly.

If she was more interested in his cars, then he could work on them at their house and wouldn't have had to drive drunk.

If she had her license, he could have made her come and pick him up instead of getting into the truck.

If she hadn't left him, he wouldn't be stuck hiking all night with nothing to eat or drink.

And for that matter, if she had done her wifely duties, he wouldn't have had to kick her out of the house, and they wouldn't have lost the baby.

As these thoughts swirled through his mind, fueling his anger and drive to keep going, doubts crept in like they always did. He thought back to his foster dad and the time he had tried to run away. He hadn't gotten past the driveway before the garage door opened, lighting the driveway where he was trying to hotwire the family car.

After the beating, he had sworn to Soledad that he would never be like their foster dad, no matter what. And he had tried. For months after getting married, he had tried. But Rosaria just never got anything right, and then he had to punish her. He didn't want to, not really. But how else would she ever learn?

He felt shame wash over him but he pushed it away in favor of the anger. Anger was more comfortable. Anger allowed him to blame his wife. Shame fueled his drinking, and drinking fueled his anger. He didn't know how to break the cycle.

When she had announced she was pregnant, he was overwhelmed. He didn't know how to be a father. In truth, he was scared that he wouldn't be a good father, although he would take that secret with him to his grave. The only father he had ever known was the one he had sworn never to be like. But he knew of no other way.

"You should have never married her," he said. "There were so many other girls."

He crested the ridge as the sun rose and scanned down the far side for any sign of his wife. The sun warmed his back. He turned around to look back at their trailer, but the sun was too bright on the horizon.

If Doug and Scott had found their truck and done what they had promised, Santiago should be checking on the house in an hour or two. Then it would take him some time to get a search party organized. The search and rescue team would probably scour the mountain on foot and horseback, but could potentially call in a chopper. Either way, he needed to find his wife quickly—before they did.

"Where are you?" he scowled.

\*\*\*

As if she had heard him ask the question, Rosaria turned back to look up the hill. Rocks and trees blocked her view, but she knew that Jorge was back there somewhere. He wouldn't stop until he found her. And this time, he might not bother dragging her back home.

She found a creek bed and groaned. It was dry as far as she could see, it being so late in the season. Come spring, it would run fast and clear, but she didn't have until spring. She found that hiking down the center of the creek was easier than weaving through trees and over rocks, and she made good time.

She reached a small dry waterfall and climbed out of the creek bed to scramble down the banks to the bottom. As she grabbed onto the branch of a pine tree, a handful of needles pulled free in her hand. Without thinking, she stuck the needles in her mouth and began to chew. The taste was strong, and the needles poked at her cheek, but chewing helped produce saliva to wet her dry tongue and lips.

*Tastes like Christmas*, she thought. The smell drew her thoughts back to her first Christmas with Jorge when they were seniors in high school and inseparable.

*"I got you a present," Rosaria said as she stood back and watched Jorge work under the hood of his baby—an old El Camino he had saved up to buy.*

*Jorge held out his grease covered hand. Rosaria stepped back. This is not how she had imagined this going. She wasn't going to hand him the perfectly wrapped package with his hands like that.*

*"10mm socket," Jorge said.*

*"Oh," Rosaria responded, laughing inwardly at herself. Of course he hadn't been paying attention to her, not while he was working on his baby. She searched the socket set balancing on the radiator until she found the one marked 10mm and handed it to him.*

*Without acknowledging her, he clicked in the socket and began ratcheting a bolt somewhere deep in the engine well. He looked sideways and stretched his arm so that he could get a better angle on the bolt. He had a little spot of grease on his nose. He closed his eyes, concentrating fully on turning the ratchet.*

*Rosaria giggled and pulled her phone out of her pocket to snap a picture. The flash went off and Jorge jumped in surprise, knocking his head against the hood.*

*"Ow! What do you think you're doing?" he yelled. He swore and held a dirty hand over the bump, wincing in pain.*

*"I'm sorry. I'm sorry. Are you okay?"*

*"No, that freakin' hurt. Why are you taking pictures anyway? Do something useful for once."*

*Rosaria felt hurt, but told herself he didn't really mean it. He was in pain. She had just handed him the socket after all, hadn't she?*

*"Sorry, babe. You were just cute with the little spot of grease on your nose and everything."*

*"Cute, huh? You want some of this?" He stepped forward with his arms outstretched, his pain suddenly forgotten.*

*"Ew, get away," she laughed playfully. "You're too dirty."*

*"I'll show you dirty," he replied suggestively, wrapping her in his arms.*

*"Stop, you're getting grease on my outfit," she protested.*

*He held her tighter and tried to kiss her.*

*"Jorge, stop it," she said and pushed him away. The wrapped present fell out of her hand and dropped to the concrete, smashing in one corner. She heard the contents shatter. "Oh no, look what you did," Rosaria said. "Your present is ruined."*

*"Look what I did? Look what I did?" His voice rose in volume. "Look what you did." He pointed to the cut on the top of his head. Blood oozed from the wound.*

*"That's not what I meant. Sorry."*

*"Just go," Jorge said, walking into the garage. He ran a shop towel under the laundry sink faucet and held it to his head.*

*Rosaria followed him inside. "Here, let me," she offered, reaching to take the wet towel from his hand.*

*He slapped her hand away and barked. "Go home.*

*"But..."*

*"Get lost!"*

*"Fine," Rosaria cried and spun on her heels.*

*When she got home, Rosaria sprayed the grease on her clothes with stain remover and threw them in the wash. She wrapped a clean towel around herself and went upstairs to her bedroom and threw herself on the bed. She had worked so hard on the present for Jorge and now it was for sure broken; she had heard the unmistakable sound when it fell.*

*"That's it; I'm done," she told her teddy bear. "I don't know why I even try. I always screw everything up; I can't do anything right. What is wrong with me?"*

*Her door opened and Alejandra crept inside. She sat next to Rosaria on the bed. "What's wrong?" she asked gently. She ran her fingers through Rosaria's long hair.*

*"I ruined it again," Rosaria explained.*

*"He didn't like your present? But it's so cute."*

*"He never even opened it." Rosaria sat up and explained what happened.*

*"It's not your fault," Alejandra said.*

*"But I know he doesn't like me taking his picture without asking."*

*"You're his girlfriend. You're allowed to take a picture of your boyfriend."*

*"You just don't understand."*

*"No, you're right. I don't understand. You need to just dump him." Alejandra was starting to get angry.*

*"But I love him."*

*Alejandra sighed. "I know you do, sweety," she said more gently.*

*"I just don't like to see you upset all the time like this."*

*"It's okay. I'm fine. I promise."*

"Red flag number eight hundred and two, is it?" she said, her mouth full of chewed up pine needles. She spat them out and ran her tongue over her teeth.

She climbed back down into the creek bed at the base of the small falls and continued down the hill, careful not to roll her ankle on any of the river rocks.

***

Alejandra waited at the trailer while Officer Gonzalez worked on his phone and the radio. It wasn't long before every patrol vehicle in town was parked haphazardly in the front yard.

An older man with a bushy gray mustache climbed the steps and entered the trailer. The others immediately stopped talking, giving him their full attention.

"Chief Austin, this is Alejandra, uhm," Officer Gonzalez began, leading Alejandra forward.

"Santos," Alejandra said. "Alejandra Santos." She shook the Chief's hand firmly. "I'm Rosaria Castro's little sister."

Soledad burst through the door at that moment. "What's going on? What happened?"

Chief frowned. "Woah. Woah. Who do you think you are?"

Soledad looked around the room, panic in her eyes. When she found no sign of anyone hurt or in trouble, she turned back to the Chief. "I'm Soledad Castro, Jorge's sister"

Alejandra raced over to Soledad and took her hands. "Do you know where she's gone?"

"No, I don't. She left a note saying she was going to your house over the weekend, but I figured that she was just trying to give herself time to get away."

"So, you don't think Jorge did anything to her?"

Soledad felt the urge to protest, but she unfortunately understood Alejandra's concern. "He was in jail when I found the note, and seemed genuinely surprised when she wasn't here Monday morning when he got out of jail."

"I need you to give your statement to one of my officers, young lady," the Chief said.

Soledad nodded. "Right, okay." She looked around at the officers in the room. All of them were dressed in uniform except for a dark-skinned man in his mid-forties.

He nodded at her and stepped forward.

"My name is Abraham. Abraham Malone, ma'am. I'm the detective assigned to this case."

"What case? Is there a case?" Alejandra asked.

Detective Malone held out his palms. "Just a missing person's case at the moment. We have to open a case in order to run the search and rescue operation. That's all."

"Wait, I thought you had to wait 24 hours or something before opening a missing persons case."

"That's TV ma'am. We have reason to believe there might be, uh, well extenuating circumstances."

"What does that mean?"

Detective Malone ignored her questions and continued. "Chief Austin will be in charge of the search operation while I try to figure out what happened on this end. Is there a room we can use to talk privately?"

"The nursery?" Soledad suggested.

Officer Gonzalez stepped in. "I'm sorry ma'am but that room isn't in a proper state." He turned to Detective Malone. "You can use my patrol car, sir," he said.

"Thank you, Officer Gonzalez. Soledad, is it?"

She nodded.

"Follow me please." He started towards the door and turned back. "I need to speak with you directly afterwards, Mrs. Santos," he said.

"Fine, okay," Alejandra replied. She wandered through the crowd of officers to the living room windows and looked out across the desert to the mountains beyond.

"Be careful hermana," she whispered. She turned back to the room. "We have to find her before he does," she declared forcefully.

Everyone stopped speaking and stared.

"Her life depends on it."

# CHAPTER 37
## 1849

The morning broke crisp and bright, and Rose felt a newfound determination and optimism for the future. She knew it would be hard, but together they would make it. They decided over breakfast that they would explore the flat stone a little more to see if they could get it open. But no matter what they found, they would set out the next day for Santa Fe. The deadline was fast approaching and there was no point waiting for the last minute.

Paul carried the bowie knife and Rose carried little Joseph in the sling, with the spade in her hand. The western side of the standing rock was still bathed in cool morning shadow as they got to work.

Paul began by scraping the seam with the knife. "There is actually a small gap here," he observed as he worked the knife back and forth. "It's filled with something." He pulled out the knife to examine the blade. A waxy substance covered the thin metal. He held it to his nose and sniffed.

"What is it?" Rose asked.

He wrinkled his brow as he tried to place the familiar smell. He headed the knife to Rose so that she could try.

"It's beeswax!" she cried.

"You're right," Paul agreed. "That's exactly what it is. That's very interesting."

"Whoever built this used beeswax to seal the door or lid. Very clever."

Paul took the knife back and began working with increased fervor. Someone had gone to great lengths to protect whatever was hidden beneath the stone.

He worked for hours on his knees, bent over with the knife. The sun chased away the cool shadow until its heat beat down on Paul's neck. But he was a man possessed. Rose let him work as she began going through their possessions to pack what they would take with them the following day.

She forced him to stop and drink every so often and placed a cool damp neckerchief on his neck to protect it from the sun and heat of the day.

"Got it!" he finally exclaimed just after noon.

Rose heard his shouting from the cabin and hurried to join him. When she arrived, he placed both hands on the stone and pushed. The stone refused to move. He took the spade and wedged it into a crack. He pulled down with all of his weight on the handle and the stone groaned as it moved first one inch and then two. Bit by bit the stone slid sideways, making a high pitched grinding noise as dry stone ground against dry stone.

Cool damp air escaped the cavernous hole below. Rose dropped to her knees and helped him push until the edge of the stone just overlapped the lip of the hole.

"I can't see anything. It's too dark," Paul said.

"How deep do you think it is?" Rose wondered.

"Go and grab the lantern," Paul said. "And a rope. We can lower the light down."

Rose hurried to the cabin to gather the lantern and some rope as Paul stretched his aching shoulders, the pain and stiffness from bending over so long finally hitting him.

"Are you okay?" Rose asked when she returned.

"Yes, just a little sore," he replied. He tied a knot in the rope around the lantern's handle and then carefully lit a candle. He waited for some wax to melt and dripped the hot wax in the candle holder before setting the candle in place. He closed the glass door to protect the flame. Carefully, he held the light over the dark hole and slowly started playing out the rope.

"There's a ladder leaning against this side," Rose said. "It looks old." She reached in and tested the first rung with her right hand. Joseph squirmed in the sling and she cradled his head with her left hand. "It feels sturdy and dry," she said.

The ladder was made of piñon branches lashed together with leather straps. "I can see the bottom," Paul said.

Rose leaned over and watched as the beam of light illuminated a stone floor. The lantern touched down, and Paul gave the rope some slack as he tied it off to the top rung of the ladder.

Rose began undoing the baby sling.

"What are you doing?" Paul asked.

"I'm climbing down to see what is down there," Rose explained. "You can't really do it." She took the baby from her chest and kissed him on the forehead before handing him over to Paul. She turned around and hiked up her skirt. She reached down with her right foot and gingerly tested her weight on the first rung—it held. "Feels solid enough."

Paul bounced the baby gently in his arms as he watched Rose step down with her other foot. She stood for a moment, waiting to see if the rung would hold. The leather straps creaked under her weight, but held. Carefully, Rose made her way down the ladder to the cavern floor below.

When she reached the bottom, she picked up the lantern and held it out at arms length. She turned in a circle. "What is this place?" she whispered.

# CHAPTER 38

## 2024

Rosaria stumbled out onto the valley floor, focused on the rock formation ahead. "I just need to reach that rock," she told herself.

She no longer even had the strength to pick up her feet as she walked, and her toes dragged in the sand. She removed her coat as the day grew warm in the valley. She walked in a trance, focused only on the blurred image of the standing rock in the distance.

She didn't even notice when her fingers fell open and released her coat from her grasp. Even holding on to something so light had become too much to bear. The coat fell to the ground and she trudged on, leaving it to bake in the sun.

Her toe caught on a rock and she stumbled forward, falling roughly to her knees. The ground beneath her seemed to undulate; her head spun. She grew dizzy and clenched her fingers in the loose sand for some sort of stability. She felt bile in the back of her throat and retched. Pain seared through her dry throat and she spat into the sand. Her vision blurred and her arms gave out. She collapsed face first into the sand, her right arm awkwardly stuck underneath her torso.

\*\*\*

Alejandra stepped outside onto the landing and watched the buzz of activity in the front yard. She nodded at Soledad who still sat in the passenger seat of the patrol car speaking with Detective Malone.

Two trucks drove up the driveway pulling trailers. One pulled off to the right. Its long flat bed trailer carried four all-terrain vehicles. The driver parked as a group of men began undoing straps and attaching a ramp to the back of the trailer.

The second truck pulled off to the left, parking on a patch of dry grass. It pulled a large horse trailer. The side windows of the trailer were open and Alejandra could see the brown snout of one of the horses peeking out of the window.

She smiled and walked down the steps. Horses were something she could relate to. They always calmed her, and she knew they would help ground her amidst the buzz of unfamiliar activity going on around her.

The driver climbed out of the truck, fitting a straw cowboy hat on his head. He noticed Alejandra's approach and nodded.

"Mrs. Santos is it?" the man said.

Alejandra looked up in surprise. "How do you know my name?" she asked.

"I was at the auction in Amarillo last weekend as well. You and your husband got that sorrel mare I had my eye on."

Alejandra looked more carefully at his weather worn face and felt a spark of recognition. She smiled. "That's right. I remember you. You almost got us on that one," she said.

"Give me a hand?" he asked as he walked to the back of the trailer.

"Sure."

He unlocked the back gate and swung it open. "Ted Swenson," he said and held out his hand.

"Good to meet you Ted." His hand was calloused and rough. "Thank you for coming to help."

"Always glad to work these ladies," he said. He glanced over at the other trailer. "Despite all of that technology, horses are still the best way to get through those mountains."

Alejandra smiled.

"What's your job here? You on the search and rescue team?"

Her smile faded. "It's my sister who's missing," she explained.

"Oh, I'm so sorry," he said as he climbed up into the trailer. "Don't you worry. We'll find her."

# CHAPTER 39

## 1849

"What is it?" Paul asked. "What do you see?"

"Get me another candle," Rose said. "I'll try and light the room so you can see."

Paul used the side of the standing rock to push himself to his feet, Joseph cradled over his shoulder. He grabbed his crutch from where it leaned against the rock and tucked it under his arm.

"In fact, grab whatever candles we have left," Rose said. "You need to be able to see this."

"I'll be right back."

Paul returned a few minutes later, and Rose climbed the ladder to take the bundle of candles from his hand. She opened the little door of the lantern and used the flame to light the other candles. She placed them around the room, sticking them to the rock with melted wax. The room gradually revealed itself.

Paul knelt at the entrance. "I don't understand," he said.

The underground room was larger than he had expected, cut into solid rock. The red rock walls were smooth from eons of the water's gentle cutting. At the deepest end, a small pool of water shimmered under the candlelight. A steady stream fell from a hole in the rock about two feet up from the pool's surface.

Rose placed her hand in the cool water and swirled it around. "It's ice cold," she said.

"Where does it come from?"

"It appears to be some sort of natural well," she said. She reached over the pool and touched the rock wall at the back just above where the water fell into the pool. "I can feel it," she said. "I can feel the water moving inside the rock. The wall must be thin."

"Is that what feeds the pool up top?" Paul asked.

"It must be," Rose replied.

She wandered out of view for a moment as she explored another section of the cavern. A shelf of rock was cut high into the wall in a dark corner. Rose reached up and ran her hand over the surface. She felt her hand bump up against something hard and angular, wrapped in what felt like animal hide. She patted the surface but couldn't tell what it was. She went up on her tiptoes and tried to drag the object closer to the edge of the shelf where she would be able to grab it.

"Come on, come on," she said.

"What is it?" Paul asked, frustrated that he wasn't able to join her down the ladder.

"I don't know, but there's something on a ledge up here that I can't quite reach."

"Is there something you can stand on?" Paul asked. His knee nudged a small stone, and it crashed to the cavern floor, the thud echoing through the room.

"You scared me," Rose said, holding a hand to her chest.

"Sorry."

Rose walked toward the opposite end of the cavern to search for something she could use to stand on, but paused mid stride when she felt the ground vibrate. The pool of water rippled in concentric circles. She listened intently. "Do you hear that?" she whispered.

"No, what...?"

"Shhh."

They both strained to hear. The vibrations grew stronger and the rumble of hooves gradually grew louder.

"Someone's coming," Paul said.

"Hurry, hand me the baby," Rose ordered.

"What? Why? It could be help."

"Or it could be something else." Memories of the horse thieves flashed through her mind. She climbed the ladder and reached out her arms. Paul placed Joseph in her outstretched hands.

"I'll go see who it is," he said.

"First, push the lid closed behind you."

"What? No!"

"Paul, just do it. We'll be safe here. When they leave, come back for me."

"Are you sure?"

"Yes."

The rumble of riders had grown louder. They were close. Rose heard one of the men call out to the others.

Paul looked around, hoping to find another option, but the ground was nothing but sand. Finally he sighed and pushed the stone cover back into place using the shovel for leverage. When only a crack was left visible he stopped. "There," he said. "I'll leave it open just a crack."

"Anybody home?" They heard a voice shout from the other side of the rock.

Paul hurriedly brushed sand over the stone to camouflage it and stood.

"Coming," he yelled.

"Who's there? The voice demanded.

Paul's voice faded as he rounded the corner. "Name's Paul Callandish," he said.

Rose waited at the base of the stairs, her heart racing and her mind conjuring up possible scenarios, every one worse than the previous. Their meager nest egg was sitting out in plain view on the makeshift table. She had removed the money from its hiding place as she was preparing their packs to leave. The coins sat in a small cloth drawstring purse—it was all they had left in the world.

# CHAPTER 40

## 2024

The first team of searchers raced across the desert on their ATVs while another group climbed into the back of a pickup truck to be driven to the base of the mountain. Soledad exited the patrol vehicle and motioned for Alejandra to take her turn.

Alejandra was torn. She desperately wanted to join the searchers but knew it was important for Detective Malone to truly understand the severity of the situation. They had to find Rosaria before Jorge did.

The two women passed each other in the yard and paused for a second.

"Did you tell him the truth about your brother?" Alejandra asked quietly.

They didn't look at each other, each understanding the potential repercussions of their statements.

"He's my brother," Soledad whispered weakly.

"He'll kill her. And you know it."

Alejandra heard Soledad swallow a sob. "Not everything," she finally admitted. "But I told him enough to know it's bad."

Alejandra nodded and walked ahead. Soledad wiped her eyes on her sleeve and walked to the backyard to watch the ATVs make their way across the desert. She prayed she had done the right thing. Was it worth losing her brother to save Rosaria? Jorge was the only family she had.

Alejandra ducked into the passenger seat of the patrol car. Detective Malone was writing furiously in his notepad and didn't notice she was there until she coughed politely to get his attention. He looked up.

"Oh, sorry. Mrs. Santos, thank you for speaking with me."

"How can I help?" Alejandra asked.

Detective Malone looked down at his notebook and flipped to a clean page. He wrote her name at the top and then checked his watch before writing the date and time. Alejandra tapped her foot impatiently on the floorboard.

"Tell me about Jorge and Rosaria's relationship," he finally said.

Alejandra exhaled. "That's a lot of ground to cover," she said. "Where do you want me to start?"

"Wherever you think is relevant," he said. "I need to know everything I possibly can about what might be going on here."

"Okay, well, then get comfortable. This may take a while."

Detective Malone pushed his glasses up on his nose and held his pen poised over the notepad, prepared to listen.

***

Rosaria awoke to a sharp pain on her neck just beneath her ear. She opened one eye and heard wings flutter in her ear. Everything was blurry, and she blinked rapidly to try and clear her vision. Her eyelids felt like sandpaper scraping across her corneas.

A black form began to take shape, slowly coming into focus. The form jumped and cawed loudly. Rosaria recognized the call of the raven and shuddered. *It must have thought I was dead*, she thought.

She tried to speak, but her throat was too dry, and it came out as croak. "Go away."

The raven cocked its head and hopped closer.

Rosaria assessed the situation. She couldn't feel the arm tucked under her body. She struggled to roll enough to pull it free. She grimaced at the pins and needles as blood started to flow again through her arm.

Something moved closer to her head and she readjusted her focus. The bird blurred in the background as a scorpion came into view. It crawled nonchalantly along the desert floor, its tail curled high over its body, ready to strike at the first sign of a threat.

*How long was I out?* she wondered. She struggled to formulate her thoughts. Everything felt jumbled in her head.

*Jorge! Where was Jorge?*

She managed to roll onto her back and stared up into the deep blue sky. She squinted against the brightness of the day and groaned. She hurt all over, but nothing seemed to be broken. Her backpack pressed against her back, making that position uncomfortable. She grunted and pushed herself up into a sitting position.

The raven cawed in protest at her apparent resurrection and took to the air. It circled over her once, then flew up into the sky.

"Thanks for the wake up," Rosaria said dryly. She felt something wet trickle down her cheek and reached up to touch it. She stared curiously at the bright red blood coating her fingertip as she struggled to make sense of what happened. "The raven," she said, finally connecting the sharp pain that had woken her up with the cut under her ear.

She struggled to her feet. The world spun in circles around her feet, and she felt another bout of nausea threaten to overcome her. She closed her eyes and focused on breathing deeply. Slowly, the ground beneath her came to a stop and she found her equilibrium.

The backpack felt heavy, weighing down her shoulders. She shrugged it off, letting it fall to the ground. She considered just leaving it, but thought better. She leaned down and unzipped the pack to rummage through the contents. She found the pocket knife and slipped it into her jeans pocket. Next, she unclipped the empty water bottle. She fumbled with swollen fingers to click it onto a belt loop.

She took one last look at the pack and made her decision—the remaining items would just have to stay. She took her first unsteady step and paused to find her balance before taking the next. She felt a shiver roll through her body and cold sweat break out on her forehead.

"Don't think about it," she said. "Just focus on the rock." She looked up to get her bearings and took another step forward, and then another.

She found it difficult to remain focused, and soon her mind wandered back to the day they graduated from high school. The graduation ceremony was held in the morning, and the graduating seniors had plans to go out to the reservoir to swim and celebrate that afternoon. Rosaria was excited to spend the day with her friends.

*She walked outside after Jorge's third time impatiently honking the horn of his El Camino. She felt happy and confident. She had splurged on a new bikini for the party and had done her hair up the way Jorge liked it.*

*"Hold your horses," she laughed as she walked down the sidewalk.*

*Jorge scowled but didn't respond. She skipped across the yard and gave Jorge a peck on the cheek before stepping up to the passenger side door of the car. Jorge didn't move from where he was leaning against the hood.*

*"Where do you think you're going like that?"*

*"What do you mean, babe? We're going to the lake with everyone else. Like we talked about."*

*"Like that? You think I'm going to show up at the lake with my girlfriend looking like that?"*

*Rosaria looked down at herself. She had a tank top on over the bikini and a sarong tied around her waist. She carried a bag with towels and sunscreen in the crook of her elbow.*

*"What do you mean?" she asked, feeling confused and disappointed at his reaction. She had thought he would like it.*

*"What do I mean? You just think I'm going to let you waltz around the lake with the entire senior class watching you dressed like a slut?"*

*Her heart dropped and her hands began to shake. "Jorge, you don't mean that. It's just a swimsuit."*

*"Go inside and change. Put some clothes on. You know better."*

*"I thought you would like it. I bought it for you."*

*"Go. Now."*

*"Babe."*

*"Go!"*

*Rosaria dropped the bag to the sidewalk and walked back to the house, her shoulders slumped in embarrassment and disappointment. Hot tears streamed down her face. She went up to her bedroom and changed out of the bikini into her old one piece suit. She pulled on a pair of jeans and a t-shirt over the suit, her discarded bikini lying abandoned on the floor.*

*When she returned outside, Jorge was sitting behind the wheel. The bag was in the back and the radio volume was turned up too high to carry on a conversation. He looked her up and down and*

*nodded his approval before she climbed inside. He roared away*
*before she even reached back for her seatbelt.*

\*\*\*

Jorge made his way down the back slope of the mountain, half running, half sliding. He knew he had to make up for lost time if he was going to find her before the search party did.

He walked through various scenarios in his head as he went, trying to plan what he would do when he found her and what he would say when the search party caught up.

He thought back to the true crime documentaries Rosaria liked to watch. He had always complained about them, but was now starting to appreciate her forcing him to watch with her. Little had she known that she was helping him formulate his plan.

He heard a raven caw in the distance and looked up to see it circle around something on the ground and fly away.

*Must have been scared off by a coyote or something*, he thought. He knew ravens were carrions and would eat from animal carcasses. But he didn't think they would fight a coyote, not alone.

He slid down a hill of loose rocks and swore when he felt a small pebble in his shoe. He tried to kick it free, but it just lodged itself deeper in the toe. He didn't want to stop, but the pebble started scraping against his big toe and he didn't have a choice. He found a boulder to sit on and untied his work boot. He shook it free and scratched the bottom of his foot.

His sock was soaked through with sweat, and his foot was sore from so much walking. It felt good to let his feet breathe for a moment. He looked down the trail and made a quick decision.

"Just for a minute," he said. He untied the other boot and dropped it to the ground. He pulled off both socks and swung them around in the air to try and dry them out. He wiggled his toes in the sunlight as he studied the path ahead.

"What is that?" he asked, peering into the distance. Far out into the valley, something moved. It was too far to make out, but it was clearly moving. He grinned maliciously. "Is that you Rosaria? I think it just might be."

He pulled on his socks and slipped into his sweaty boots, his discomfort all but forgotten. He was getting close.

# CHAPTER 41

# 1849

Paul rounded the rock to find an entire platoon of cavalry at their front door. A half a dozen mounted men looked him over with curiosity. Four saddles stood empty, and he heard a commotion behind him. He turned toward the house.

An officer stood in the doorway watching as his men searched the cabin.

"Excuse me, sir," Paul said.

The officer turned around. "Lieutenant Baker," he said.

"Lieutenant Baker. Yes. My name is Paul Callandish. May I help you?"

Lieutenant Baker looked at Paul's crutch and down at his foot. "What's wrong with you?" he asked.

Paul took a step to the side to try and see what the other men were doing in the cabin. Lieutenant Baker moved to block his view.

"What is it you are looking for?" Paul asked.

"This isn't a conversation, Mr. Callandish. Answer my question."

Paul hopped back in surprise at the officer's bluntness. "Yes, sir. I, uh, rattlesnake. We, I mean I, was a part of the last wagon train with Captain Adams and they left me behind to die, actually."

"I remember the train. That was a while back. How long have you been here?"

Paul thought for a moment, remembering the impending Apache deadline. "About five weeks now," he said.

An enlisted man emerged from the cabin holding a pocket watch in the air. Lieutenant Baker took it by the chain and rested it in his palm. He spent a moment inspecting the watch before turning his attention back to Paul. "Where'd you come by this?" he asked.

"It belongs to Sgt. Whitmer," Paul replied honestly. "I'm hoping to return it to his family when I get to Santa Fe."

"What do you know of Sgt. Whitmer?" Lieutenant Baker barked. He stepped towards Paul with a hand on the hilt of his sword.

Paul held up both hands. "Let me explain."

Another soldier emerged from the cabin, and Paul saw him tuck a small bag into his pants pocket. "Hey! That's mine!" Paul yelled.

Lieutenant Baker turned to his soldier and held out his hand. The soldier scowled at Paul and sullenly drew the pouch from his pocket. The coins jingled as the bag hit Lieutenant Baker's palm. "I apologize for Private Setter, here," he said. "I'll hold on to this for you to keep it safe."

"No, I can keep it safe. Thank you," Paul said, holding out his hand.

Lieutenant Baker ignored him and dropped the bag of coins into his coat pocket.

"Hey," Pvt. Setter said. "Where's yer horses?"

"That's what I'm trying to tell you. Sgt. Whitmer and Pvt. Jones chased a band of horse thieves to the house and, well..." Pvt. Jones' death flashed through his mind.

"And?"

"Yes, well, they were both killed and the horses stampeded. So, I'm stranded here until my foot heals up enough to walk to Santa Fe."

Lieutenant Baker scowled as he assessed Paul's story. "You say they were chasing horse thieves?"

"Yessir. The horses wore the US brand."

"Did you get the names of the thieves?"

"I'm sorry; I don't recall."

"Bill by chance?"

"Yes, yes, that was it."

"Lieutenant!" one of the mounted men cried, pointing to the cross marking Sgt. Whitmer's grave.

Lieutenant Baker strode over to the site and squatted down to read the carving on the wooden cross.

"Where's Pvt. Jones?" he asked. He pushed down on his knees and stood.

Paul thought about his wife hiding in the cavern and decided he did not want the soldiers looking around back there. "His body was with the horse thieves where we were settin' to bury them. But that big storm blew through and their bodies washed away in a flash flood."

Lieutenant Baker eyed him suspiciously. "You want me to believe that Bill, his gang, and Pvt. Jones all just disappeared in a flood and the so-called stolen horses ran off into the desert?"

"That's what happened."

"And you just happen to have Sgt. Whitmer's property in your possession as he's conveniently dead and buried right here?"

"I don't understand what you're trying to say," Paul admitted.

"What I'm saying is that you colluded with Pvt. Jones to murder Sgt. Whitmer and then helped him become a deserter from the United States Army."

Paul shook his head, trying to follow Lieutenant Baker's logic. "If I were in on it with Pvt. Jones, why would I be stuck here without a horse?"

Lieutenant Baker laughed dryly. "Because you made a deal with the wrong man. As soon as he got what he wanted, he took off and left you stranded. You're lucky he left you alive."

Paul felt anger welling up in his chest. He desperately wanted to tell Lieutenant Baker what really happened, but something was off. He did not trust the man enough to let him know that Rose and Joseph were hiding in the cavern.

"Lieutenant Baker, I swear. I was just here recovering from my snake bite when Bill and his gang rode up bein' chased by Sgt. Whitmer and Pvt. Jones. I was lucky I didn't get hit. Look. You can see the bullet holes in the wall there."

Paul pointed at the house, and the last soldier from the inside inspected the wall. "I see the holes, sir. The place got shot up something fierce."

"See?" Paul said.

"All I know is that one of my best men is dead and buried and you are in possession of his property," Lieutenant Baker said coldly. "Pvt. Setter, arrest this man."

Pvt. Setter stepped forward and yanked Paul's hands behind his back. His crutch fell to the ground. Paul struggled to get his arms free, but he was no match for the soldier.

*I have to let Rose know what is happening*, he thought desperately.

"You can't arrest me. I've done nothing wrong!" he yelled.

Rose stood on the ladder with her ear pressed against the small opening. She hadn't been able to make out any of the conversation until Paul yelled. She cried out, and covered her mouth. "Paul," she moaned. "No, no, no!"

"You're making a mistake," Paul yelled.

"Shut him up," Rose heard a man say.

Paul struggled to stay upright on one good leg with his hands behind his back. He cried out in pain as Pvt. Setter yanked on his arm to keep him upright as he tied his wrists together. The rough rope bit through his wrists, and he felt blood trickle down his hands. He took a deep breath to yell again, but before he could say anything, he felt a searing pain slam into the back of his head. The world went black and he slumped to the ground.

"That'll shut him up," Corporal Taylor said as he wiped blood from the butt of his pistol. He slid it back into its holster and helped Pvt. Setter to lift Paul's unconscious body into the saddle of one of their extra mounts.

Lieutenant Baker grabbed the reins of his horse and put his foot in the stirrup. "Burn it down," he said as he swung himself into the saddle.

Rose set Joseph on the ground and climbed back up the ladder. She bent over and pushed her shoulders up against the stone lid. She pushed up with all of her strength. "Come on. Come on," she grunted as she strained against the weight of the stone, but it didn't budge.

She couldn't get the right leverage she needed to push the stone out of the way. Despite knowing it was useless, she refused to stop. Again and again she pushed until the smell of smoke finally filtered down through the crack.

Joseph began to wail and so, exhausted and defeated, she climbed down to the cavern floor and took him in her arms.

# CHAPTER 42

## 2024

A lejandra finished her interview just as another truck and trailer pulled into the driveway. With nowhere else to park, the driver pulled onto the spotty front lawn.

"Jose!" she cried.

Detective Malone looked up from his notebook in surprise. He glanced over at the trailer and then turned his attention back to his notebook. Alejandra had told a compelling story of violence and abuse stretching back to high school.

He finished the last line and shut the notebook. He wrapped the attached elastic around the book and slipped his pen in his front pocket. He pinched the bridge of his nose. He felt a headache coming on and wondered if he still had some ibuprofen in the glove box of his unmarked car.

Alejandra ran to the driver of the new truck and embraced him tightly. The man kissed her forehead before looking up at Detective Malone as he climbed out of the patrol vehicle. Detective Malone stretched his back and popped his neck.

Alejandra took the man by the hand and led him to Detective Malone. "This is my husband, Jose," she explained. "Jose, this is Detective Malone. He's the one assigned to Rosaria's case."

"Good to meet you, Mr. Santos," Detective Malone said as the two men shook hands.

"What's the status?" Jose asked.

"We think she's out there in the mountains somewhere," Alejandra replied.

"Your wife has given me a detailed statement regarding Rosaria's relationship with her husband. I'm sorry that we haven't done anything to help her sooner."

"You can't help someone who hasn't asked for it," Jose said.

Detective Malone nodded.

"What are you doing here?" Alejandra asked. "I didn't know you were coming."

"Well, I heard from Ted Swenson that he was helping with the mounted search, so I loaded up our horses and drove out here. I figured you would be itching to help."

"I am! I can't stay here just waiting."

"Well, I'm going to brief the Chief with what I've learned so far," Detective Malone said, excusing himself. "It was nice to meet you, Mr. Santos."

"It's just Jose. Nice to meet you too."

Detective Malone walked back to the trailer as Alejandra followed her husband to the horse trailer. Her gray spotted Appaloosa gelding nickered as soon as he saw her, and she climbed into the trailer to say hello.

"Ted said he was going to start where the trail ends on this side of the mountain, so I'm thinking that we drive over the pass and start our search on the western face. What do you think?"

"She's been gone since at least Sunday morning, so it is possible that she has made it over to the other side. So yeah, that makes sense. We can meet in the middle."

"Okay, good. Do you need to tell Detective Malone that you're leaving?"

"He didn't say that but it's probably a good idea. I'll grab my coat from inside as well. Did you pack supplies?"

"Of course I did," Jose replied.

"You're the best," Alejandra said as she stepped down from the trailer. She leaned in and gave Jose a kiss, then wrapped him in another tight embrace. "I'm so worried about her."

Jose turned the truck around in the yard while Alejandra spoke to Detective Malone. As they drove through town and turned onto the old highway to drive over the pass, Alejandra watched the mesquite bushes flash by on the roadside and thought back to her sister's wedding day.

*"Are you sure?" Alejandra asked Rosaria for the tenth time. The two sisters were alone in the bridal room down the hall from the pastor's office.*

*Rosaria slapped her gently on the shoulder. "Why do you keep asking me that? If I wasn't sure, I wouldn't be here."*

*"I know. I know. It's just..."*

*"Alex. I'll be fine. He loves me."*

*"He sure has a funny way to show it sometimes."*

*"Stop it. This is supposed to be the happiest day of my life. I don't need you trying to ruin it."*

*"Okay, I'm sorry. I will keep my mouth shut and smile for you. I just want you to be happy."*

*"I am. Okay?"*

*Alejandra looked down, afraid that she wouldn't be able to stop herself from saying what she really felt. Rosaria lifted her chin with a gentle touch and looked her directly in the eyes.*

*"I'm happy," she insisted.*

*Rosaria was radiant in her elegant ball-gown-style wedding dress. It hadn't been her first choice, but despite not being pre-*

*sent, Jorge's wishes seemed to have pervaded the dressing room when they had gone shopping. Where Alejandra thought the bride should be able to pick out what she felt beautiful in, Rosaria had insisted it was more important to make her new husband happy.*

*"You look beautiful," Alejandra said. She stepped back and took Rosaria in. "It was the right choice."*

*Rosaria giggled and twirled around. The two sisters laughed and Alejandra stepped in for a hug, careful not to smudge any makeup.*

*"I love you, you know," Alejandra said.*

*"I know. I love you too."*

*Alejandra grew more serious. "And I will always be here for you. No matter what. Okay?"*

*Someone knocked on the door and pushed it open.*

*"They're ready for us," their dad announced. "Wow. You look beautiful!"*

"Earth to Alex. Hello?" Jose said. He reached over and gently squeezed her arm.

"Huh? Oh, sorry. I was lost in thought, I guess."

"What were you thinking about?"

"Rosaria's wedding day, actually." She chuckled. "What a day."

"Yeah, I remember," Jose said. "It was only our second date after all."

"And you were a great sport about it, babe. Most guys would have been freaked out getting asked to a wedding on a second date."

"Well, if I'm honest, I was a little freaked out," he joked.

She playfully slapped at his arm and he pulled away, jerking the steering wheel.

"Careful! Eyes on the road, buddy."

"Do you remember the reception? That was wild."

Alejandra's lighthearted mood fled at the memory. She turned back to stare out of the window.

"I'm sorry, babe. I didn't mean to..." Jose put both hands on the wheel and exhaled. He silently berated himself for bringing it up.

*The wedding ceremony was beautiful and everyone followed the bride and groom to the reception in a friend's backyard. The happy couple greeted their guests in a reception line until Jorge began to complain that he was bored and wanted a drink.*

*"This is a party, isn't it?" he said to Rosaria.*

*She shook hands with one of their guests and then turned to Jorge. "There's still a line," she whispered.*

*"Who cares?" he replied loudly. "The line's done people," he announced.*

*As the people in line looked at each, unsure what to do, and confused with Jorge's breach of protocol, Rosaria felt her cheeks grow hot with embarrassment.*

*"I'm sorry, everyone. We haven't had anything to eat since this morning, so we would like to take a little break." She rushed to catch up with Jorge, who had already left the line behind. A woman she recognized from church gave her a sympathetic smile, which somehow made things worse.*

*Alejandra had been standing next to Rosaria in the line as her maid of honor and she followed the couple to the food table. Jose saw her leave and excused himself from the table where he had been forced to make small talk with her distant relatives to eagerly join her.*

*"What's going on?" he asked.*

*"Jorge just decided he was done with the line," Alejandra explained.*

*She watched as Jorge piled food on a plate and grabbed two bottles of beer from a neatly arranged stack of different varieties. He popped the top of both bottles and handed them to Rosaria to carry for him.*

*As Rosaria followed her husband to the table holding his two beers, Alejandra made up a plate of food for Rosaria to eat, all the while desperately trying to remain calm. They hadn't even been married a day and Jorge was already treating her sister like a servant.*

*The evening got worse instead of better. Jorge took advantage of the bar and was never without a bottle in his hand. When they announced that it was time for the couple's first dance, he drunkenly took Rosaria by the hand and guided her out to the dance floor. If it hadn't been for Jose offering to hold his beer while they danced, Jorge would have never let it go.*

*As expected as the night grew late, Jorge grew more and more drunk, which made him loud and obnoxious. Alejandra watched* in dismay as her sister repeatedly tried to get him to stop drinking and quiet down. She never found out what Rosaria finally whispered in Jorge's ear, but whatever it was, he jumped to his feet and stuck his finger in Rosaria's chest.

"If I had known this was what marriage was going to be like, I'd have stayed single," he slurred. "Nag, nag, nag."

He pushed the chair back. It teetered on two legs until gravity won over and it crashed to the ground. He walked away as a silent crowd watched in horror. Tears streamed down Rosaria's face. It was the last straw for Alejandra. She stepped forward, fully prepared to give Jorge a piece of her mind, but before she could say anything, Rosaria rushed past. The sisters exchanged looks and Rosaria shook her head in a silent plea for Alejandra to stay out of it.

Rosaria caught up to Jorge as he reached the edge of the pool. "I'm sorry, babe. You're right. Just come back and sit with me, okay? It's our wedding."

Alejandra grimaced at Rosaria pathetic pleadings. She turned away, unable to watch it anymore.

As soon as her back was turned, she heard a splash and the crowd gasped. She whipped back around. Jorge was stumbling off into the darkness, and Rosaria stood chest deep in the pool, her wedding dress floating in a halo around her, her mascara running down her cheeks.

Alejandra's stomach was tied in knots, the way it always was when she thought about that night. She wiped her eyes and looked determinedly at her husband.

"We're going to find him, and we're going to make sure that he never hurts her again."

"Of course we'll find her," Jose said.

"No, him. We're going to find him. And if I have anything to do with it, he will never be able to hurt her ever again. Do you understand?"

Jose took his eyes off the road to look at his wife. Her face was set in stone, and fire burned in her eyes like he'd never seen before. He felt a chill ripple down his spine. "Never again," he agreed. His mind went back to their kids at home, his job, and their life together. Whatever happened, he wouldn't let Jorge destroy those as well.

# CHAPTER 43

## 1849

Paul came around to the jolting bounce of a horse trotting beneath him. He turned awkwardly in his saddle and saw that they had crossed the valley and were entering the pass. His heart filled with panic.

"Stop!" he cried.

The men ignored him, thinking he was just once again proclaiming his innocence. They'd heard enough of that already.

With his hands tied to the pommel, he couldn't control the reins but he tried anyway. "Woah, girl," he whispered to the horse. She obeyed and stopped in her tracks as the others continued on.

"My wife and child are trapped," he yelled. "We have to go back."

"Heeyaw," Cpl. Taylor yelled as he slapped Paul's horse on the rump to get her going again.

"I hid them in a cavern in the rock when I heard you coming," Paul continued. "They'll die there if we just leave them."

Lt. Baker raised a hand to halt the patrol. He turned his horse and rode back to where Paul was riding in the middle of the group. "You say nothing of a wife and child while we are there but now that we are leaving the smoking ruins behind, you suddenly decide to mention them?"

"Yes. I'm sorry. I was trying to protect them. I didn't know who you were."

"Then why, pray tell, did you not say something once you saw who we were?"

"You refused to listen to me, took my money, arrested me for a crime I didn't commit, and knocked me senseless," Paul replied angrily. "I never got the chance."

Lt. Baker's eyes narrowed at Paul's blustering accusations. "Hmmm," he said. "How do we know that this isn't some sort of trick? What sort of man would trap his wife and child in a cave?"

"A murderer, that's who," Pvt. Setter said.

"Please. They'll die!"

"I don't believe you," Lt. Baker finally decided, not realizing or caring that his words were a likely death sentence for Rose and Joseph.

"Please," Paul sobbed. "Just let me get them out. Then I'll come with you. I won't cause any other problems. I promise. Please."

"Stop blubbering, man," Lt. Baker said with disgust, returning to the front of the platoon.

"Rose," Paul sobbed. "Forgive me."

***

Rose fell asleep with Joseph cradled in her arms. When she awoke, most of the candles had burned themselves out, and she chided herself for not thinking ahead and saving them. She peered up the ladder at the night sky peeking through the thin crack.

"I've been asleep for hours," she said.

With her remaining candle, she decided to conduct a more thorough search of the cave, hoping there was another way out. At the far side, a rock protruded from the wall, hiding a small room behind it. From the cavern, it was difficult to see.

Rose walked around the rock wall and held the candle out in front of her. Her mouth dropped open in shock. By the dim light of the candle, she could see a roughly constructed cot covered in a uniquely patterned wool blanket. She stepped closer. Next to the bed stood a small table made with wooden legs and a thin stone top. She approached the table and realized that there was some sort of scroll set neatly at the back of the table against the wall.

She set Joseph down at the foot of the bed and sat down next to the table. She set the candle down and picked up the scroll. It felt dry and brittle in her hands. Carefully, she untied a leather thong from around the scroll and worked the knot free. The thong immediately broke where it had been wrapped in the knot, and the scroll began to unroll in her hands.

She set the scroll on the table and partially unrolled it. She squinted in the dim light. The ink had faded over time and was barely visible. The markings were unlike any she had ever seen before, and the characters were small and densely packed onto the surface. She ran her hand over the surface of the scroll and wondered what it could be made of. It felt like some sort of skin but was so thin and smooth that it could only have been made by a skilled craftsman.

It was then she recalled the object on the ledge on the other end of the cavern. She placed the scroll on the bed next to her and tested the weight of the side table. It was heavy, but she could manage it. She lifted it a couple of inches off the ground and walked awkwardly across the cavern, her legs splayed wide.

With the table placed under the ledge, she carefully stepped up. The table wobbled under her weight, so she quickly grabbed the bundle from the shelf and stepped down. Leaving the table there, she rushed back to the little room to examine her find.

Joseph gurgled contentedly when she returned, and she leaned down to give him a kiss on the forehead. She sat next to him with the bundle on her lap and began to unwrap the oiled leather.

Her eyes widened in surprise as the contents of the bundle came into view. A small sword sat on top of a stack of thin stone tablets. She held the sword up to the light and ran a finger across the face of the blade. The metal was smooth and cool to the touch. She held the blade at an angle and ran it down her arm, where it easily shaved a bald spot. "Still sharp," she observed.

She set the sword down and picked up one of the tablets. The stone was the same as the rock walls of the cavern, but had been skillfully broken into thin tiles. She ran her fingers across the surface of the top tile and felt the indentation of carefully carved characters.

She grabbed the scroll and placed it next to the first tablet. Holding the candle with her other hand, she studied the writings on the scroll and carvings on the tablet. They appeared to be an exact match.

She sat back against the wall and closed her eyes to think. "Who was here?" she asked. "And what are these writings?"

She pictured a man, huddled over the table with a carving tool, carefully transcribing the scroll onto stone. Who was he? Where did he go?

"It's a mystery, Joseph," she finally said. "But it's not our concern at the moment. Right now, we have to either wait for daddy to get back or figure out a way out of this place. We can worry about the mystery later."

Joseph cooed in response, and Rose smiled.

# CHAPTER 44
## 2024

Rosaria stumbled out into the middle of the road. The pot-hole pitted asphalt ran as far as the eye could see in either direction, its painted lines faded in the desert sun.

"I made it," she whispered, but she felt no sense of triumph or accomplishment. The road was clearly infrequently traveled, in even worse shape than most roads in the state. There was no telling when someone else would drive by.

Her legs gave way and she slumped to the hot asphalt. Sitting with legs crisscrossed in the middle of the road, she contemplated her precarious position. She knew that she couldn't walk any further. Her body was shutting down from exhaustion and dehydration. She struggled to think straight. If someone didn't come soon, she would die.

"At least I will die free, and not because of Jorge," she mumbled. *But it is because of Jorge,* a little voice in her head argued. *If it wasn't for him, you wouldn't have been forced to escape through the desert. Don't let him off the hook so easily.*

The little voice sounded just like her sister.

"That doesn't matter now," she argued. "At least it's on my own terms."

*I told you that you could come to me. I would have helped you.*

"I know sis, but I couldn't put you in danger any longer."

*Do you still love him?*

Rosaria's eyes had drifted shut but they jerked open at this question. She examined her heart. Did she? "I don't know," she finally admitted. Her eyes drifted shut again and her body swayed back and forth.

*"We're moving," Jorge announced when they returned home from their honeymoon.*

*"I know. I can't wait to decorate our apartment," Rosaria replied. They had gone out together before the wedding and found a small one bedroom apartment over a drug store. It was small and old, but Rosaria was excited to have a place they could call their own. They were at Jorge's foster parent's home until they could move into the new place at the beginning of the month.*

*"No. I canceled the lease. We're moving back to be near my god-father. He found me a good job."*

*"But Jorge, that's a couple of hours away from my family. When will I see them?"*

*"I'm your family now," he said angrily.*

*"I know that, babe. But I still want to see my sister. She's my best friend."*

*"Did you not listen to the preacher? Cleave unto your husband, remember?"*

*"I know. I am, but..."*

*"Honor and obey."*

*"Yes, of course, but we should have talked about this first. You can't just decide things like this. We're a team now."*

*"It's my job to provide for this family, and that's what I'm doing. It's a good job and I've made my decision. Pack your things. We leave tomorrow."*

*"Wait. Tomorrow?" Rosaria slumped to the couch in shock.*

*"Soledad lives there too. She can be your friend. Come on. Get up. You have a lot to do. I put some boxes on the back porch."*

*He grabbed his keys from the little tray on the coffee table.*

*"Wait, where are you going?" Rosaria cried.*

*"I'm meeting Matteo. I've got some stuff to do." He opened the door.*

*"You're not going to help me?"*

*He walked out, slamming the door behind him.*

Rosaria smiled wanly. "I should have listened to you from the start, Alejandra."

The raven circled above her, then landed on the road in front of her. It hopped on the hot pavement as it examined the strange human sitting in the middle of the road.

"Go away," Rosaria said weakly.

It cawed again and hopped closer.

*You've got to move. Go. Don't give up now,* the bird seemed to say.

Rosaria examined the bird and touched the scratch below her ear. The blood was dry and the cut scabbed over. "Wait, were you trying to hurt me, or are you protecting me?"

"Caw, caw!" the bird cried.

"All right. All right," Rosaria said. She slowly got to her feet.

The bird took to the air and flew towards the standing rock, which jutted up from the valley floor not far from the road. It perched on top of the formation and cawed in encouragement as Rosaria stumbled her way to the rock.

# CHAPTER 45

## 1849

They camped for the night in a small meadow just off the trail, but Paul found no way to escape. They kept his hands bound and, with his bad leg, he couldn't get far. The men were disciplined soldiers and set up a perimeter, with guards assigned watches throughout the night.

Paul tried to sleep, but between the discomfort of being bound and worry for Rose, he was never able to get comfortable. He spent the night praying and trying to figure out a way to escape.

As the sun rose, the camp came alive. The men coughed and growled for coffee as they packed. They chose a spot near Paul to relieve themselves, and he turned in disgust as they each took a turn.

Pvt. Setter brought him a biscuit and a cup of coffee, which he consumed gratefully. His eyelids felt heavy from lack of sleep, and the coffee helped to wake him up.

A rider hailed the camp. He rode in trailing a lead rope attached to a line of horses behind him.

"Lt. Baker around?" he asked the guard.

"Chet, what brings you here?" Lt. Baker said from near the campfire.

Chet dismounted and handed the reins to the guard. The guard stepped aside to let Chet pass.

"I found these horses back up the trail a ways and was bringin' 'em back to Fort Leavenworth for the reward money."

"Reward?" Lt. Baker asked curiously.

"Most of 'em carry the Army brand, and isn't there a standing reward for the return of any stolen Army mounts?"

"I think you're right."

"Better believe I'm right. Anyway, I saw your camp here and decided to collect now instead of going all the way back to the fort."

"Let me have a look."

All of the men's attention was directed toward the line of horses, so as Lt. Baker approached the line of horses, Paul followed, hopping on one leg.

Chet showed the men the US brand on the first horse and Lt. Baker nodded.

Paul looked further down the line and recognized the white spot on the forehead of one of his team immediately. "Hey, those two in the back are mine," he said.

All of the men turned their attention to Paul, and the soldier who had been assigned to watch him rushed forward and grabbed him by the arm. The sudden movement pushed Paul off balance, and he fell face first to the ground. The men all broke out in laughter as his guard helped Paul back to his feet. His nose was bleeding, but he seemed unharmed otherwise.

"Can you prove it?" Lt. Baker asked.

"They're both branded with the Rockin' C," Paul replied.

Chet went to the back of the line to check the two animals. "Rockin C," he confirmed.

"And they ain't wearing saddles because they were in the corral when the thieves came."

"Hmm," Lt. Baker said.

"Hey, look!" Cpl. Taylor cried. "That's Sgt. Whitmer's mount. And there, that one is Pvt. Jones'."

"You sure?"

"Yes, sir," Cpl. Taylor replied.

"Looks like your story checks out, Callandish."

Paul forced himself to refrain from speaking the words running through his mind and instead just nodded.

"Untie the man," Lt. Baker ordered.

Paul rubbed his raw wrists. The men watched as he awkwardly hopped down the line of horses to his own. He wasn't the best horseman and wasn't used to riding bareback, but he would make it work.

As he was trying to figure out how to mount the horse, he remembered the small purse of coins.

"Lt. Baker?"

"What is it?"

"My money, if you please."

Lt. Baker failed to hide his disappointment that Paul hadn't forgotten. He pulled the purse from his jacket pocket and held it in a tight grip. "You owe Chet here a reward for rounding up your horses." He tossed the bag to Chet, who snatched it out of the air with a greedy smile.

"The Army pays a dollar for every head," Chet stated.

Paul gasped and eyed him suspiciously. That was a fortune. "In that case, Lt. Baker owes you seven dollars, right?"

Lt. Baker gave Chet a dirty look. He knew that if he paid a dollar per head to Chet, everyone would expect that much. He would never get reimbursed for that either. "I'm sure you misheard the man, Mr. Callandish. The Army pays a half dollar for every head, not a dollar."

Chet frowned, but didn't argue. He took a silver dollar from the pouch and tossed it to Paul.

"Could someone help me up?" Paul asked. "My bad foot and all..."

All of the soldiers laughed and returned to their duties in camp, leaving Paul wondering how he would pull himself onto the horse. Chet walked over and took pity on him.

"What's wrong with yer foot?" he asked as Paul settled onto the horse's back. Chet untied the horse from the line and handed Paul the lead rope to the second horse.

"Snake bite. Rattler," Paul replied.

Chet grabbed the horse's mane. "Wait, that's you?"

"What do you mean? How do you know about me?"

"I ran into an Apache scout I know and he told me about the white man who survived a rattlesnake bite. Well, I'll be."

"Apache?" Paul felt his heart race as he tried to remember what the moon looked like the night before. He had been so focused on escape that he hadn't even thought to look. "What was the moon last night?"

"Huh?"

"The moon, man. How close are we to the new moon?"

"A day at most, I'd guess," Chet replied, confused.

Paul kicked the horse's flanks, and Chet stumbled backwards as the horse shot forward.

"What in the Sam hill?" Chet exclaimed.

"Sorry," Paul yelled over his shoulder as he turned the horses onto the trail and set them into a gallop.

***

Rose paced the cavern in darkness as she waited for the morning light to filter through the crack overhead. Joseph slept peacefully on the old bed. With the sword in hand, she climbed the ladder. She wedged the sword in the crack and positioned her shoulders to push upwards as she leveraged the sword against the lip of the opening.

With all her might, she pushed upward as she pulled on the sword. The motion was awkward in the cramped space, especially as she was trying to maintain her balance on the ladder, but the stone finally moved an inch, then an inch more.

She yelped in surprise and redoubled her efforts. Progress was slow, and she had to take frequent breaks when pains started shooting through her back, but the stone was moving.

During one of her breaks, she heard movement above her and she began to shout without thinking that it might not be her husband.

The lid was open enough that the sword no longer helped with leverage, so she tucked it in her apron strap behind her back. She pushed up against the rock again and took a deep breath before pushing upwards with her legs. To her surprise, the stone slid completely away. Caught off guard, she fell backwards and just barely caught herself by falling against the lip of the opening.

"Paul!" she cried, sure he had come back to free her. But the words caught in her throat when she saw the three Apache scouts standing before her. She took a step down the ladder and they stepped forward in unison.

"My baby," she said. She made a cradling motion with her arms and pointed back into the cavern.

The leader nodded and she rushed down the ladder to retrieve Joseph, all the while frantically trying to figure out what to do. *Is our time up already?* she thought.

She returned to the base of the ladder with Joseph in her arms and looked up. The three men stood tall over the entrance staring down at her. With a deep breath, she climbed the ladder. As she reached the top, one of the scouts stepped forward, blocking her from being able to climb out completely.

"Baby," the lead scout said, holding out his arms.

"No, I'm fine. Thank you." She tried to ascend the next rung, but one of the men put a hand on her shoulder, stopping her from being able to climb higher.

"Baby," he said again. "I help."

Rose saw no other option, so she held Joseph out to the leader and he snatched the baby into his arms and stepped back. The others stepped back as well, allowing her to climb out of the hole.

"Thank you," Rose said.

The three men eyed her ominously.

"You no go," the leader said. "New moon." He pointed to the sky.

"We tried, but my husband was kidnapped and I was stuck down there, and we lost our horses, and he still can't walk." She finally stopped talking when she realized they probably didn't understand anything she had said.

She held her arms out for Joseph, but the lead scout stepped backwards and the other two blocked her path.

"Give me my baby," she said, her voice trembling. She leaned forward and the two scouts stepped in even closer. "He's my baby. Give me my baby. I'll go.

Right now. Just give me my baby." Rose felt panic welling up inside her. Her voice shook as she felt herself losing control.

The lead scout looked down at the baby. His eyes widened in surprise. "Big medicine," he finally said. He looked at Rose and shook his head. "You no go. Now my baby."

"No!" she shouted.

He turned and began walking away with Joseph in his arms. "Joseph!" she cried. "You bastard!" Anger overtook her and she rushed forward, surprising the two men. One grabbed her arm. A primeval wildness overtook her in her desperation to save her son. She reached behind her back and withdrew the sword and slashed at the scout holding her by the arm.

He screamed in surprise and pain. The sword cut his bicep to the bone, and his arm hung limp and useless at his side. Rose swept the sword to her other side. The second Apache jumped back to avoid the blade, but the tip cut a line across his chest.

The two experienced fighters quickly recovered from her surprise attack and advanced. She swung the sword wildly, keeping them at bay, but they advanced in unison, forcing her back. She jabbed at the man to her left. He sidestepped the attack and brought his club down on her forearm.

She heard the bone crack before she felt the shock of pain, She screamed and the sword clanged to the ground. She saw him swinging the club at her a second time, and instinctively she ducked away. The club missed her head, but hit her squarely on the shoulder.

Every inch of her wanted to lie down and surrender, but she looked past her attackers to the man calmly holding her son and felt renewed strength and determination flow through her.

She screamed and rushed the man to her right. She clawed at his face as he tried to fight her off with one arm. Her thumb found his eye and she pushed. He yelled in pain and punched her in the side with his good arm. She grunted, but held tight, refusing to stop the attack.

His partner grabbed her from behind and wrapped his arms around her body, pinning her arms to her sides. The pressure against her broken arm would have caused even the strongest man to faint, but she no longer felt any pain. She was a woman possessed.

She wriggled and kicked, screaming like a wounded wildcat, but she couldn't break his grasp. In a last ditch effort, she jerked her head back and felt the shock of her skull connecting with the scout's nose. His grip loosened for just a second, and she dropped out of his arms and spun around. She rammed her good shoulder into his stomach and plowed forward.

Her brain barely had time to register how close she was to the hole in the ground when she felt the cold steel of the sword slice through her back. She looked down in shock at the tip of the blade sticking out of her stomach. With one last effort, she pushed the man to the edge of the hole. He teetered on the edge, but his momentum couldn't be stopped. As he fell back, he grabbed a fistful of Rose's dress. The fabric ripped away, but it was too late.

Her forward momentum combined with his pull was too much too overcome. Rose fell forward through the entrance, landing face down on top of the scout. He stared up at her with dead eyes and nightmare images of Pvt. Jones flashed through her mind. She struggled to roll off of him, as darkness began to cloud the edges of her vision.

***

Paul galloped into the camp and released the lead rope. He turned his horse around the rock and jumped to the ground, not even thinking about his bad foot. He didn't even realize that his foot took his weight as he ran to the underground cavern. The stone was pulled closed, just as he had left it.

"Rose, I'm here. Rose, are you okay?"

He heard a groan from below through the narrow opening.

"Rose, I'm coming!"

The spade was still leaning against the rock where he had left it. He wedged the blade into the hole and pulled down with all of his strength and weight. The stone moved, and he dove to the ground and pushed it the rest of the way, all the while telling his wife that he was there and they were safe.

When the stone lid was pushed off far enough for him to get to the ladder, he stopped pushing and swung his legs over the side. He half slid, half climbed down the ladder.

The sun was high in the sky and the light shone directly into the cavern. He stared in confusion at the scene. An Apache man laid on his back, his eyes open and unseeing. His wife lay next to the Apache on her stomach. Blood pooled under her, deep red under his shadow.

He frantically turned her over, and she groaned in pain. She coughed, and he noticed blood staining the corners of her mouth. He took her in his arms and pulled her close to his chest.

"Rose. No. Rose, it's me. You can't die."

Tears stung his eyes and he struggled to breathe. He didn't know what to do. The front of her dress was so soaked in blood that he couldn't see where she was wounded.

"Rose. Wake up, darling. Stay with me."

Rose's eyelids fluttered open and she smiled weakly. "Paul," she whispered.

Paul suddenly remembered the baby. "Joseph! Where's Joseph?"

Rose frowned and looked confused, like she couldn't quite recall what happened.

"Darling. Where's the baby?"

She suddenly remembered and her eyes opened wide in terror. "The Apache," she croaked. "They took him."

He glanced at the dead scout and then up at the sky. He felt her squeeze his hand and he looked into her eyes.

"Find him," she said.

"We'll find him together. You're going to be alright."

Rose reached up with her good arm and placed a bloody palm on his cheek. He took her hand and kissed it gently.

"Find him," she repeated.

"I promise," he replied, tears streaming down his face.

She nodded slightly and closed her eyes.

"I love you," he whispered.

He thought he saw her smile through his tears.

When his tears finally stopped, he leaned down and kissed her cold lips.

# Chapter 46

## 2024

Rosaria reached the rock but wondered what to do next. The raven still sat perched at the top of the formation, looking content that it had done its job. With one hand on the rock, she stumbled around the base, searching for something she could use that would help her.

She stopped for a moment in the shade of an old piñon pine at the back of the formation, but something pushed her forward and she continued her search. As she rounded the corner back to the front, she looked out over the desert and saw a figure coming towards her.

She couldn't make out any details, but didn't need to. She knew it was Jorge.

Panic washed over her and her heart began to race. "What do I do, bird?" she asked.

The raven cawed and took flight.

"Maybe he hasn't seen me yet, and I can hide behind the tree." She saw movement out of the corner of her eye and turned to look. The hem of a woman's skirt disappeared seemingly into the rock face itself.

"Now I'm seeing things," she said as she walked in that direction.

A yucca plant grew up against the rock face where the vision had disappeared. Rosaria pushed it to the side to examine the ground behind the plant for tracks or any other sign that she was hallucinating. To her surprise, she found an opening in the rock, just wide enough for her to slide into.

She glanced up and saw the face of a woman staring back at her. The woman quickly moved away up the narrow crevice.

"Hello?" Rosaria cried. "Can you help me?"

Wind whistled down the crevice, but no one answered her call.

She climbed carefully, still weak and unsteady on her feet. When she reached the top, she stepped over a rock and found herself in a flat area surrounded by rocks. The woman was nowhere to be seen. She stepped forward cautiously, wary it was some sort of trap.

She smelled the cool taste of water first, and didn't believe her eyes when the catch basin came into view, full of clear water. She dropped to her knees at the edge of the basin and thrust her arms into the pool to make sure that she wasn't dreaming.

The cold water sent a chill down her spine, but she lifted her arms out to ensure they were truly wet. Water dripped from her elbows and she began to laugh and cry. She cupped her hands and leaned down, drinking the life-saving water until she began to cough and sputter.

"Too fast," she told herself. "Slow down." She remembered hearing some-where that you shouldn't drink too much too fast if you are dehydrated. Every fiber of her being wanted to dunk her head into the pool and guzzle every ounce she could, but she forced herself to stop for a moment to digest the water she had already inhaled.

The surface of the water calmed, and Rosaria looked down at her reflection. To her surprise, someone other than herself stared back at her. The woman's hair was pulled back into a bun, and she smiled warmly. Rosaria knelt there, transfixed. The woman's eyes pulled her into their depths. She looked so familiar but Rosaria couldn't place her. She felt as though she was staring into a family portrait.

Rosaria moved her head to the side, and the woman in the reflection mirrored her movements.

"Who are you?" Rosaria asked.

The woman replied, but despite there being no sound, Rosaria was able to read her lips. She recognized the word. She had seen people speak it often enough in her life.

"Rose?" she asked.

The woman nodded.

"Me too," Rosaria said, and the woman nodded.

A warm feeling washed over Rosaria, flowing from head to toe in a wave. She felt safe staring into Rose's eyes.

The moment only lasted for a second, just until Rose's eyes widened and the warmth was replaced by terror. Before Rosaria could react, she heard Jorge growl and two strong hands grabbed her by the neck and head and pushed her face into the water.

Rosaria gasped involuntarily, inhaling a mouthful of water. She kicked and bucked, but she was weak against Jorge's strength. She opened her eyes under the water and saw Rose staring back at her, saying something she couldn't hear or understand. She screamed, but the sounds were carried to the surface by bubbles, where only Jorge could hear them.

He squeezed her neck tighter and pushed her face against the wall of the basin. Rosaria reached back and clawed at his hands, but he was relentless. Pain filled her lungs as she focused on not taking a breath. She knew she wouldn't last much longer.

She watched as Rose's face faded into the depths of the pool, slowly disappearing before her eyes.

***

"You can pull off here," Alejandra said, pointing to a gravel area next to a rock formation in the middle of the valley.

"Is there a dirt road that goes up to the mountains?" Jose wondered. He took out his phone and opened a map application to study the area.

"I'm going to get some air," Alejandra said as she opened the truck door.

She opened the back door and took a bottle of water from the cooler on the seat. The water was ice cold and felt good. Her eyes felt heavy from crying. She poured some water into her cupped palm and splashed it on her face.

She walked towards the rock, mildly interested in how it came to be standing there in the middle of the valley. She had visited Shiprock before, and this formation paled in comparison, but was still fascinating to her.

"I wonder how long it's been here," she said. She reached the formation and frowned. Indentations dotted the sand around the base of the rock. They appeared too big to belong to an animal and too straight to be natural.

She began to follow the tracks, but Jose interrupted her. "There's supposed to be a dirt road about a mile ahead," he said. "Come on. Let's go."

Alejandra held out a hand to him.

"What is it?" he asked.

She beckoned for him to come over. He ensured the truck was in park and climbed out. "What do you see?" he asked as he drew close.

"Look at these tracks," she said. "The sand's too soft for any detail, but they follow in a line around the rock here. It's weird."

Jose studied the ground and walked around the corner. "They keep going," he reported. "You're right. They're too big to be a coyote or cat, and too straight, well not straight, too uniform to be from nature."

"Do you think she was here?" Alejandra asked.

Jose looked back towards the mountains. "If she is, then she made it a lot further than anyone thought," he said. He continued following the tracks, staying wide of them to avoid disturbing the trail. He wound up back where he started. "They don't lead off anywhere on the back side. It's like someone walked around the rock in a circle and then just disappeared."

"That doesn't make any sense."

"I can get the dog out of his crate, see if he can find a trail."

"Are we wasting our time here?" Alejandra asked.

"We won't know unless we try," Jose replied. "It won't take long. If there's a trail, Ole Dan will find it."

"Okay, let's do it."

# CHAPTER 47
## 1849

Paul didn't know how much time had passed as he knelt there cradling Rose in his arms, but he snapped out of his trance when he heard the whine of a coyote above him. The cry reminded him of little Joseph, and he jumped to his feet.

It was only then that he realized that his injured leg held his weight. "Thank God for that at least," he said.

He tore a strip of cloth from the hem of Rose's dress and dipped it in the water. He wrung out the dust and grime and soaked it again. Gently, he wiped the blood from Rose's face and laid her arms across her chest.

He rolled the body of the Apache into a dark corner away from his wife, leaving him unceremoniously on his belly.

"I'm sorry, Rose," he said as he stood over her body. "I'll come back for you. But for now, this is the best I can do. I won't let you down; I promise. I will find Joseph if it takes me the rest of my life."

He bowed his head and prayed intently. After saying amen, he took one final look around the cavern and climbed the ladder.

He pushed the lid closed, this time closing it completely to keep scavengers away. He took shovels of sand and dumped them over the lid before spreading it out evenly. He stepped back to ensure the opening was camouflaged and nodded in satisfaction. At least no one else would be able to find Rose's burial place before he could make it back to provide her a proper funeral.

He walked his horse around the rock to the burnt out cabin. As quickly as he could, he rummaged through the debris. Luckily the fire had burned the walls, but hadn't spread through their meager possessions. Everything was covered in soot but was mostly intact.

He found their one saddle and saddled up his horse. He collected some food and his pistol. He couldn't find the holster, so he tucked the pistol in his belt and continued searching for other items of use.

He dug a carpet bag out from under a collapsed wall and hefted it up onto the makeshift table. It was Rose's bag, and he hesitated before undoing the clasp, unsure that he would be able to hold himself together.

He reached into the bag and felt the carved edges of a small picture frame sitting on the bottom. He pulled out the little frame and choked back a sob when he recognized it. He hadn't known that Rose had brought the sketch with them.

It had been a wedding present from Rose's cousin. Although it was a simple charcoal sketch of the newlywed couple, her cousin had captured Rose's smile perfectly. Paul held it to his breast and closed his eyes as a wave of sorrow washed over him.

*"Sit still," her cousin Emma said, feigning exasperation.*

*He and Rose looked at each other and started giggling again. She made a face, sticking out her tongue, and he leaned back in laughter. The bark slipped under him and he lost his balance, flailing his arms as he fell backwards to the ground. He landed on his back with a thud, his legs sticking up in the air.*

*Rose laughed even harder, and Emma joined in.*

*"Are you okay?" Rose asked between gasps.*

*"Fine," Paul groaned. He saw the hilarity of the situation, and*

*soon he was overtaken with laughter as well.*

*"Maybe I will just sketch you like that," Emma said. "Your boots sticking up in the air."*

*"What is going on out here?" Emma's mother, Vera, demanded. She stepped out of the back door, wiping her hands with a kitchen towel, her apron covered in evidence of her baking marathon for the wedding. She was supposed to be chaperoning the couple but had placed those duties in Emma's lap.*

*"Is the couple behaving?" Vera asked.*

*The two girls looked at each other, to Paul, and back to Vera before breaking into laughter once again.*

*"A little help here?" Paul begged.*

*"Serves you right," joked Rose. She leaned over and took Paul by the wrist. She tried to pull him up, but he was too heavy and instead she lost her balance and fell over the log on top of him.*

*The laughter began again as Rose rolled away and stood. She brushed off her dress and fixed her hair as Paul struggled to roll over. He finally managed to roll backwards onto his knees and got to his feet.*

*"It looks like a circus back here," Vera said sternly.*

*"Sorry, Mother," Emma said. "I will take my duties more seriously."*

*"Hmph,"* Vera replied. *She returned back to the kitchen and smiled slyly once her back was turned, recalling the day she was married.*

*"Can we please sit for five minutes?"* Emma asked. *"Otherwise, my drawing will look nothing like you."*

*"Yes. I'm sorry,"* Paul said, *brushing dust and grass from his waistcoat. "I will be serious. I promise."*

*Rose sat on the log and arranged her dress, pushing away any wrinkles. Paul sat next to her, but not too close. They weren't married yet, after all.*

*As Emma sketched, Paul slowly walked his hand across the log until his pinkie brushed up against Rose's hand. He felt a jolt of electricity at the touch. They kept their hands touching, frozen in place, until eventually Rose's finger twitched, and she placed it on top of Paul's hand. It was all the invitation he needed. Without moving his upper body or making any move that would give them away, he took Rose's hand in his own and squeezed.*

*When Emma announced that she was finished with them, Paul excused himself to help with the chores at home and Rose went inside to help Aunt Vera with the pies.*

*The wedding day arrived, and Emma presented them with the framed sketch after the ceremony. Paul was shocked. It was so lifelike. He had never known that Emma was so talented. They immediately placed the drawing on their mantle for all to see.*

When he opened his eyes again, he pushed his pain away and stuffed the portrait into his saddle bag. "Joseph needs me now," he said.

He had very few possessions, but he didn't need much. He rounded up the second horse and tied the lead rope to the pommel of his saddle. He swung up into the saddle and took a last look around the place where his son had been born.

He clicked his tongue, and the horse began walking. He had no idea which direction the Apache scouts had gone, but he guessed they were returning to camp, so they would be going the opposite way from how they had left the camp a month earlier. It was just a guess, but Paul was no tracker and couldn't think of anything better to do.

As he reached the foothills, he turned in his saddle. The rock formation was visible in the distance. "I'll be back," he promised.

He turned his back on the standing rock, his temporary home, for the last time.

# CHAPTER 48
## 2024

Jose reached into the cab and grabbed his cell phone from the tray between the seats. "Do you have Detective Malone's number?" he asked.

"What?"

He walked around the front of the truck and tried again. "Do you have Malone's number?"

Alejandra jogged up to the truck. "I have his card," she said. She reached into her back pocket and pulled out a business card. "Why?"

"I think we need to notify him that we may have found something. And we need something belonging to Rosaria for the dog. I was going to grab something at the house, but completely forgot."

"Oh, dang. I didn't even think of that."

Jose took the card from Alejandra and began dialing Detective Malone's number. A raven cawed and landed on the hood of the truck with something in its beak. The dog was in his crate back in the trailer, but he began barking furiously.

Jose set down the phone before pressing the send button. "What is that?" he asked. He reached out towards the bird, but the Raven cawed in protest and hopped back.

Alejandra rounded the truck to stand next to her husband so she could get a better look at what the raven carried in its beak.

The raven hopped forwards towards Alejandra. In one smooth motion, it dropped the object and took flight.

Alejandra reached for it. "It's a sock," she said. She studied the cartoon characters on the ankle sock, trying to understand its significance if anything.

"That was weird," Jose said. "I've never seen a wild raven give something to a human like that."

"Wait! Rosaria has socks like this. I knew they looked familiar."

"Serious?"

"Yes, hurry. You need to call Detective Malone and have him search Rosaria's dresser to see if these socks are there or not. If not, this could be hers."

"He's going to think we're crazy."

"Just tell him we found it, not that a raven mysteriously delivered it to us."

"Right. Okay."

Jose made the call as Alejandra went to the back of the trailer. She released the bolt and swung the doors open. The dog barked in anticipation.

"Hey boy," Alejandra said. "We need your help, okay?" Dan barked and wagged his tail. He was ready and eager to go to work.

*** 

The anger overtook him as soon as he saw her kneeling at the pool, and he forced his wife's head into the pool before he even knew what he was doing. A small part of him warned him that he should stop, that he was going too far, but he pushed the voice to the side.

He squeezed harder and clenched his teeth. As she bucked and fought him, he felt a surge of energy wash through him. "I should have done this years ago," he found himself saying. He cursed Rosaria as she fought for her life, squeezing harder the more she fought. All of the times she had defied him, all of the times she had disobeyed him, all of the times she had embarrassed him—they all flashed through his mind.

The memories justified his actions. His throat cried out in thirst, but he couldn't even stop long enough to drink. He was compelled to keep going. He couldn't stop.

He didn't notice that Rosaria had grown limp, or that the water suddenly receded in the pond.

When he finally realized that she was no longer moving, he looked down. Confusion filled his mind. His sleeves were soaked through. Her hair was wet. But the pool was dry. He released his grip and shook his head, trying to understand what he was seeing.

At that moment, Rosaria gasped for breath. The sudden noise startled him, and he fell back onto his bottom, releasing his grip on her. She sputtered and coughed.

"How are you...? How is this possible?" he whispered in awe. He crossed himself and looked heavenward for answers.

Rosaria wretched and spewed water into the dry basin. She pushed herself up and wiped the hair out of her eyes. She was still gasping for breath, and recoiled when she saw Jorge sitting there staring at her.

"You're alive," he stated.

She stumbled back and pushed herself to her feet.

"I'm free of you," she declared. "Go. You are nothing to me."

Jorge felt his anger returning, replacing the shock of her recovery.

"You can't leave me," he said. He got to his feet and took a step towards her. She stepped sideways, keeping her back to the rock face.

"You're my wife, till death do us part." His lips curled in a malevolent smile.

"I already have," she said. "I don't love you," she said, surprising even herself at the admission. "It's true," she continued. "I don't think I ever have."

"Nice try," he sneered. "You know you could never leave me. No one else would want you."

Rosaria felt the familiar twinge of doubt creep into her heart. He knew exactly what to say. Was she worthy of someone's love? Was Jorge the only man who would take her?

She looked past him, and her eyes widened in surprise. Rose stood behind Jorge. She wore an old-fashioned dress that fell to her ankles. She nodded her encouragement and smiled.

"I don't need someone else to want me in order to matter," Rosaria finally said. "I'm enough."

Jorge looked surprised. Rosaria had never talked this way before.

"You don't actually believe that." He stepped toward her and she sidestepped again. "Anyway, it doesn't matter if you do. You aren't leaving this place alive. And when I find your poor dead body with the search team, I'll cry and put on such a show that no one will even think that I could have killed you. It's perfect. You did me a favor by running away."

Rose stayed behind Jorge and encouraged Rosaria to keep moving, so she followed along. With one hand against the rock face behind her, she made her way around the small plateau. She eventually left the safety of the rock at her back and stood in front of the pool while Jorge now stood against the rock. Rose smiled and held out a hand for Rosaria to stop.

As she did, Rosaria heard a sharp rustling noise coming from a crack in the rock behind where Jorge stood.

Jorge tilted his head. "What's that noise?"

# CHAPTER 49
## 2024

Detective Malone hung up the phone and stuffed it in his pocket. Chief Austin waited to be updated.

"Mr. and Mrs. Santos may have found something."

"What?"

"They found a sock they believe might belong to Rosaria. They want me to check her dresser to see if it's there or not."

"A sock? How can they know it's her sock?"

"It has a cartoon character on it, so I guess it's pretty unique."

"Well, the bedroom's a mess, so I'll get an officer to help you with the search."

"Thanks, Chief."

Detective Malone pulled a pair of gloves from his back pocket and put them on. He walked back to the master bedroom and sighed. "This is going to take forever," he sighed.

"What are we looking for?" the patrol officer asked behind him.

Detective Malone described the sock.

"At least it's a bright color," the officer said.

"That's one thing," Detective Malone agreed.

\*\*\*

Alejandra took the leash down from the hook on the trailer wall and bent down to open the dog crate. She clicked the leash onto Dan's collar and led him out of the trailer just as Jose hung up with Detective Malone.

"What did he say?" she asked.

"He's going to search the room and call us back."

"Is he going to send searchers our way just in case?"

"He didn't say that. But I think everyone they've got is up on the mountain. So, if he doesn't find the socks, I'm guessing he'll head out this way himself."

*** 

"This is ridiculous," Detective Malone said as he dropped another item of clothing onto the growing pile in the corner.

"What is?" the officer asked.

"I'm going to head out to where the Santos are waiting. You keep searching."

"Okay, boss."

"It's going to take an hour to get there, even if I'm running code. So there's no point waiting here until we end up going out there anyway."

"That sounds logical to me."

"Have you heard any updates from the search teams on the radio?"

"Just that one of the teams found the entrails of what they think was a mountain lion. Looks like poachers."

"Great, just what we need—a bunch of criminals up on the mountain with the search team."

"Right?"

"Okay. Keep searching and call me as soon as you find anything, or don't, I guess. I'll tell the Chief I'm leaving."

"Roger that."

# CHAPTER 50
## 1849

T he Apache scouts rode into the camp late that night. The baby had cried nonstop since leaving the standing rock, and the lead scout decided to push on through the night to get him to a wet nurse as soon as possible.

The entire village awoke to the sound of the baby crying. His wife approached and took the baby from him without a word. He dismounted and left his horse with his son to care for.

The other women surrounded his wife, eager to get a glimpse of the pale faced baby, curious to know the story. He ignored their questions and continued to the chief's wikiup. As he passed the home of the deceased scout's family, he motioned for the father to join him.

The chief had heard the commotion and stood outside. When the scout approached, he welcomed the two men inside.

The scout began by telling the story of the white man who had survived the bite of the snake, and the pregnant woman who cared for him. They had been living at the base of the sacred waters.

"Where is my son?" the father asked.

"Patience."

"Why did you not kill them or force them to leave then?" the father asked.

"They had strong medicine," the scout replied. "He deserved an opportunity to leave. She held the rattle of the snake who attacked him."

The chief nodded, gesturing for the scout to continue.

"When we returned, we found their home burned to the ground and heard her crying for help. The legend is true."

"What legend?"

"The legend of the ancient wanderer, who caused the waters to spring forth from the rocks."

The chief raised his eyebrows, but allowed the scout to continue.

"The woman was trapped in a cavern beneath the rock. I took her son as she climbed out and felt his strong spirit. He was born in the place of the sacred waters, son of the father who survived the bite of the snake. When I refused to return the baby, the woman went wild. She fought bravely and with honor." He turned to look at his companion's father. "Your son died valiantly, fighting against a great warrior."

"A woman?"

"A powerful woman. A warrior who also died in the fight."

The chief placed the hand on the father's knee. "You are to be proud of your son," he said.

The father nodded.

"The child is here," the scout said. "I wish to raise him as my son."

"And what of his father?" the chief asked.

"He was gone. The child has no father."

"You will raise him as your own," the chief agreed. "He is one of us now."

# CHAPTER 51
## 2024

The noise grew louder as Jorge looked around in confusion. "What's that noise? Stop that!"

"It's not me," Rosaria said.

She looked behind Jorge and watched as Rose put her hand in her apron pocket and emerged with a rattle. Rose shook the rattle at Jorge, although hers didn't make a sound.

The snake slithered out from beneath the rocks and coiled around itself. It raised its diamond shaped head as it rattled its tail in warning.

In the moment that Jorge realized the sound was coming from just behind him, he was already too late. The snake struck with lightning speed, sinking its fangs into Jorge's calf.

Jorge screamed, and the snake struck again. He kicked, trying to dislodge the snake's fangs from his leg. The snake let go, but before he could move away, it struck for a third time.

Rosaria watched in horror as the dead-eyed creature attacked her husband.

He stumbled backward and tripped over his own feet, falling to the ground. Another snake emerged from under the rock and joined the attack. Jorge twisted and turned. He tried to scramble backwards, but the snakes were too fast for him.

A third joined in, and soon his screams stopped, replaced by pathetic whimpers.

As fast as it had begun, the attack ended. Jorge lay on the ground, his breathing labored and skin flushed as the venom swept through his bloodstream.

Rosaria stood rooted to her spot, unable to move.

***

"What was that noise?" Alejandra asked. "Did you hear that?"

"Yeah. It sounded like someone screaming."

Dan barked wildly and strained at his leash.

"That didn't sound like Rosaria," Alejandra said. "Maybe an animal?"

"Possible. Let's put Ole Dan on the scent and see what happens."

Alejandra let Dan smell the sock. She then unlatched his leash and gave him the command to search. He immediately ran to the rock and completed a circuit around its base before stopping in front of a yucca plant and crying out.

"What is it, boy?" Jose asked him.

They both went to where Dan was pointing and whining. Jose used his boot to tamp down on the yucca spines, and the dog shot into a crack in the rock.

Alejandra and Jose looked at each other in surprise before Alejandra stepped in to follow the dog into the crevice.

They heard Dan's excited barks indicating that he had successfully found his prey before they reached the top. When they stepped out onto the small plateau, it took a moment for them to take in the scene.

Rosaria hardly looked like herself. Her face was gray and her wet hair clung to her neck. Her clothes were dirty and torn. She stood unmoving, an empty look on her face.

Jorge was writhing on the ground. "Help me," he cried.

Alejandra ignored his cries and stepped over him to get to her sister. As soon as she placed her hands on Rosaria's shoulders, Rosaria snapped out of her trance and fell into Alejandra's arms. "Is it really you?"

"It's me sweetie. You're all right now. You're safe."

"What happened?" Jose asked.

"He tried to kill me," Rosaria explained. "But then, he was attacked by rattlesnakes. It was horrible."

Jose protectively reached down and grabbed Dan by the collar. "Snakes? I hate snakes."

"They're gone now," Rosaria said.

"Should I call an ambulance?" Jose asked.

Rosaria and Alejandra shared a look. They shook their heads in unison.

"Please," Jorge croaked, but they ignored him.

Alejandra wrapped her arm around Rosaria and led her towards the entrance to the crevice. Rosaria looked up and saw Rose standing at the entrance. Rose smiled and placed a hand to her heart.

"Thank you," Rosaria mouthed,

"Did you say something sweetie?"

"No, nothing. I'm just so glad to see you."

When they reached the truck, Jose gave Rosaria a bottle of water while Alejandra found a sweatshirt on the back seat she could change into. Rosaria sipped on the water slowly this time.

"Do you have any food?" she asked. Her stomach rumbled.

"I have some jerky," Jose said as he rummaged through the cooler. "You need to chew it really well and eat slowly."

"I know. Thank you."

As she chewed on the jerky, an unmarked car pulled in behind the truck, its lights flashing in the grill.

Detective Malone climbed out of the car and approached.

"We found her, Detective. She's okay."

"Well, the dog found her," Jose said.

"That's excellent news. Rosaria, I'm Detective Malone. I'm so glad that you are safe. We've got a lot of people out looking for you."

"Thank you," Rosaria said meekly, embarrassed that such a fuss had been made on her account.

Detective Malone misread her embarrassment. "Don't worry. Your sister and Soledad told me everything. I'm sorry that we haven't been able to help you sooner."

Rosaria forced a smile, but didn't speak.

"So, any sign of Jorge?"

"No, detective, nothing," Alejandra said quickly,

"Do you think he could have caught up with Rosaria so soon?" Jose asked. She had more than a day's head start after all."

"Hmm," Detective Malone replied. "You're probably right."

"Did you see him at all, Mrs. Castro?"

Rosaria shook her head. "It's not Castro anymore," she said.

"I'm sorry?"

"It's Rosaria Ortega. I'm divorcing him."

"Very well. For my report, I can't change your name until it's legal. But as far as I am concerned, Ortega it is."

Detective Malone looked up at the rock formation. "These formations fascinate me," he said. "I've always meant to stop and check it out." He walked towards the rock and Rosaria looked at Alejandra, worry written on her face.

"Don't worry. He'll never find it," Jose said.

"Hey Alex?"

"Yeah, sweetie?"

"Do you remember the story Abuela told us about our ancestor?"

"Which one?"

Detective Malone touched a hand to the rock. He stepped back and took out his phone to snap a picture. A raven flew down and tried to grab the phone from his hand.

"Hey! Watch it," he cried.

The raven swooped down again and pecked at Detective Malone's head. He stumbled back out of the bird's path.

"The one about the baby boy who was orphaned and adopted by the Apache tribe. Our fourth great-grandfather I think."

"Uhm, I think so. Why? What brought that up?"

"Oh nothing."

"That's a pretty random question to be nothing."

"No really. My mind wandered a lot as I was walking, especially when I grew exhausted and dehydrated. I just..."

"Just what?"

"Did you see that crazy bird?" Detective Malone cried out. He was walking back to the cars, having given up his exploration.

"I just wondered about his mother. Who was she and what happened to her?"

"I don't know," Alejandra said.

"Never mind. It's silly."

Detective Malone returned to the little group. "I'm going to call in to the search team that you've been found, but they will continue searching for your husband. I mean, your ex-husband. Sorry."

"It's okay."

I'm sure you must be exhausted. Let's get you to the hospital and get you checked out. You've been through a lot."

Rosaria nodded. "Okay."

"You sit up front," Alejandra said. She helped Rosaria climb up into the cab and shut the door before getting into the back seat.

Jose returned from putting Dan back in his kennel with a treat for a job well done.

As Jose turned the truck around, Rosaria looked up to the peak of the rock. The sun was directly behind the formation and its rays framed the rock in brilliant shadow.

"I'm free," she whispered. "I'm finally free."

Dear Reader,

I want to say a huge thank you for choosing to read *Rattlesnake Rock*. If you enjoyed it and want to keep up to date with all of my latest releases, please consider signing up at the link outlined on the next page. You can also sign up for my monthly newsletter on my website.

In the meantime, if you loved this book, I would be enormously grateful if you would share the book with your friends and write a review. Even a mention or review on social media would be fantastic! I'd love to hear what you think, and it makes such a difference helping new readers to discover one of my books for the first time.

I love hearing from my readers.

Thanks,

Marcus Williams
www.marcuswilliamsauthor.com

Don't miss out!

Visit the website below and you can sign up to receive emails whenever Marcus Williams publishes a new book. There's no charge and no obligation.

https://books2read.com/r/B-A-FBAR-OLTDC

BOOKS 2 READ

Connecting independent readers to independent writers.

# ABOUT AUTHOR

Marcus has written thousands of pages of law enforcement reports describing the details of cyber crimes, sexual assaults, drug trafficking, and murders during his career as a federal agent. He now uses all of that "practice" to tell stories that excite, entertain, and engage. While life doesn't always have a happy ending, there is always hope found in family, friendships, and kindness.

He and his family have lived all over the world and love exploring and making friends wherever they find themselves: from California's high desert, to Sicily's historical marvels, to the beaches of the mid-Atlantic coast, to the rain-soaked forests of Washington, to the base Mt Fuji, and to the majestic Rocky Mountains. The world is full of mystery and untold stories.

Read more at https://marcuswilliamsauthor.com.

WILLIAMS & CO. PUBLISHING

Milton Keynes UK
Ingram Content Group UK Ltd.
UKHW010758110624
444053UK00004B/315